WITHDRAWN
FROM STOCK

HULL LIBRARIES
5 4072 10364936 8

Isolation Junction
Breaking free from the isolation of emotional abuse

First published in 2016
Jennifer Gilmour

Copyright © Jennifer Gilmour 2016

The rights of the author has been asserted in accordance with Sections 77 and 78 of the Copyright Designs and Patents Act, 1988.

All rights reserved.
No part of this book may be reproduced (including photocopying or storing in any medium by electronic means and whether or not transiently or incidentally to some other use of this publication) without the written permission of the copyright holder except in accordance with the provisions of the Copyright, design and Patents Act 1988. Applications for the Copyright holder's written permission to reproduce any part of this publication should be addresses to the publishers.

This book is a work of fiction. Names, characters, businesses, organisations, places and events other than those clearly in the public domain, are either the product of the author's imagination or are used fictitiously. Any resemblance to actual persons, living or dead, events or locales is entirely coincidental.

A CIP catalogue record for this book is available from the British Library

ISBN 978-1535487566

www.teamauthoruk.co.uk

Isolation Junction

Breaking free from the isolation of
emotional abuse

Jennifer Gilmour

DEDICATION

This book is dedicated to the thousands of people who find themselves, through no fault of their own, in relationships ruled by domestic abuse and to my wonderful husband, children, family and friends who gave me the courage and the means to break free and to live my life free of control.

You know who you are and I love you all.

INTRODUCTION

As a passionate advocate for women in abusive relationships, I have amalgamated and fictionalised other survivors' experiences and research alongside my own experience to write my first novel.

This details the journey of a young woman from the despair of an emotionally abusive and unhappy marriage to happiness by having the confidence to challenge and change her life and to love again. I hope that in reading my book, I will raise awareness of this often hidden and unseen behaviour and empower women in abusive relationships to seek help for themselves and to find the confidence to change their lives for the better.

The challenge is to bring about more widespread awareness of emotional abuse and coercive behaviour. My goal is for these aspects of controlling behaviour to be talked about more openly, to reach MPs and the national news for their support and to further change perceptions and policies so that people in these emotionally charged situations have a voice.

These changes are necessary to help and protect women not just from former partners but also from some of the inappropriate and inadequate decisions made within the family and magistrates' courts which, often unwittingly, leave women isolated and trapped. I appeal to all of you reading this to help 'Block the Road to Isolation Junction'.

Jennifer Gilmour

CHAPTER ONE

Ice cold rain splattered her face; her toes and fingers were numb and yet she sat there huddled up and gently rocking herself. It was a black night with no stars, like someone had just switched off the sky. The only light shining on her face was the orange glow of a single street light. Rose couldn't cope anymore, she was crying into her hands so hard it hurt her heart; it was a deep spike of a pain rushing through her body and this wasn't the first time she had felt it. Rose had felt this often through the last 5 years of her life and yet this felt like an eternity. She sat there in the mud at the front of a run-down old church surrounded by old and wonky gravestones, completely soaked through. Rose didn't care, she had learnt to become care-free from her own feelings and thoughts. It was like she had become a robot. Rose had lovely long red hair down to her bottom with stunning green eyes, a curvy figure with a peachy bottom. She used to be the centre of her family, everyone wanted to be around her because she brought life to a family gathering. She was always comical and sometimes stepping over the line, but her family and her friends loved her for who she was. Lately she had become muted at gatherings and would never go out socially unless Darren was by her side.

Rose's mind was racing through those years in which she suffered, spent and wasted with Darren. Better known as Den (a name Rose had always hated), he was a short and overweight man in his 30's. He had ended it with her, again, but this time Rose was going to act on it. This was a regular statement from Den to try and keep her in his possession by panicking her. Den didn't know that this time Rose was going to stand up to him, but how? Rose's parents had never approved of Darren simply because of the 10-year age gap.

"You're young and naive," they had said to her after the first introduction. "He's not the type of man you normally go for either," Rose's mum had expressed and she was correct. Rose did have a type and Darren wasn't her usual.

Rose had explained to her parents, "He tells me I'm beautiful and no one has ever complimented me like he does." Why hadn't she listened to them? They were correct, but Rose thought that perhaps it was good to go away from her usual type.

Why hadn't she taken the countless offers of a temporary place to stay when she became trapped?

Rose knew the relationship wasn't going to last just weeks into the mess. She thought back…

* * *

The local cinema was a weekly visit for my two close university friends Lyndsey and Helen. Together we laughed and giggled, had those stupidly drunk nights out and shared a lot of secrets that wouldn't be told to anyone outside of our triangle. Lyndsey and Helen managed to scrape some time out of me even though I had that inescapable new relationship.

Lyndsey was blonde and ditzy and couldn't be without a friend by her side; Helen was a brunette and seemed to have more fun than Lyndsey (Lyndsey seemed to always end up with her heart broken).

The three of us had just seen a comedy film. We couldn't deal with sad films and horror films were written off completely as Lyndsey would scream and scare the audience as well as get us thrown out. Laughter had over-taken all emotions and we looked like three giddy teenaged girls which was often the case when we got together! I was meant to meet Darren at the end of the film to walk back to the girls' newly rented home. However, Darren hadn't turned up; there was a text message on my phone: 'gone home' which seemed a little odd to me but I didn't think anything more of it. Lyndsey had offered to give me a lift home and so I enjoyed some more giggles with them for those last five minutes. I arrived home and was laughing on the way in; our terraced house was a small two-bed with the bathroom on the bottom floor but it was close to the centre of town and ideal for now. Darren and I both lived with housemates before moving in together and it was rushed into a frenzy when his housemates said they were moving out in a couple of weeks as they had gained jobs abroad. Darren had no one to move in with and I had come to the end of my tenancy so we were forced into a situation.

As I stepped through the small front door, it was like there was a sudden floodlight on me; the air felt cold and the room was dimly lit. Darren was sat in the armchair in the corner, slowly taking drags from his cigarette; he looked over at me like I was something stuck to the bottom of his shoe. As I always did, I began to tell Darren about how much fun I had and wondered where he had gotten to; I was looking forward to ending the evening with him which seemed like a perfect conclusion. As I talked, Darren sniggered and it took me a little while before the penny dropped.

Darren spoke in an unfriendly tone, "Seems like you've had a lot of fun without me." I was lost for words and couldn't tell where this conversation was going and why Darren was glaring at me.

"I erm, well, I always have fun with Lyndsey and Helen, it was good to catch up with them, but of course it's good to see you now." I sent a cheeky smile to him which he knew to be that special signal and I thought this might just cut through the ice but for some reason I was becoming nervous. Darren didn't look impressed and I wasn't really sure what was going on and my nerves started to show in my voice as I spoke again, "Anyway I'm tired so I'm going to get to bed."

I remember everything like it was yesterday and I wish it wasn't so clear. I walked up the stairs and ripped off my clothes and got into my pyjamas super-fast as it was the winter and I didn't want to get too cold; I had mastered this as I am anaemic and often have to jump out and into clothes in seconds. I fell to sleep rather fast as I had had a long day.

A couple of hours had gone by when I woke up in shock to Darren shaking me, "Rose, Rose, we have to sort this out!"

At first I thought there was an emergency and my heart was racing from the adrenalin. "What do we need to sort out? What's happened?" I was disorientated and panicky.

"Well, the fact that you think you can go out whenever you

want and be with whoever you want," Darren said as if I had had an affair or something.

"I don't know what you're talking about, I'm tired and it's the middle of the night." I tried to turn over and closed my eyes tightly. Darren was persistent and kept rocking me. I am one of those deep sleepers who has vivid dreams and sleep talks and walks so didn't take calmly to someone disrupting my beauty sleep at all. Darren just wouldn't leave me alone and after half an hour I was wide awake and stormed off (I often had those teenage moments). Even then he wouldn't leave me alone and persisted by following me down the stairs and I could only catch parts of what he was saying as I was focused on getting out.

"Well, that's immature,...aren't you going to talk?...I can't wait until the morning to sort this out...for fuck sake won't you just say something!"

The anger had been building in me and that was it, I got my coat on and I slipped on my trainers and walked out of the house slamming the door behind me. I remember thinking at the time what the hell was I doing and why had I let him get to me like this. It was a winter's night, cold and bitter and it had been raining and the only sound you could hear was my feet on the road with light thuds; my long hair flew behind me like a piece of fabric. It slapped me in the face reminding me of my situation. I thought a walk would clear my mind, but I heard someone following behind. 'Why can't he just leave me alone'? I was gaining more and more anger and paced faster but Darren was also doing the same and wouldn't let it lie.

I saw a cut-through some cottage houses and slipped through thinking I could get to the end and hide around the corner until he passed. No luck; I was thinking why on earth was this turning into a horror movie scene with Darren being some sort of villain. Eventually, I became out of breath with my asthma and knew I had pushed my limits when the wheezing started. I had gone around in circles around the cottages and shopping estate and finally he caught up with me.

Darren pinned me to the wall by grabbing my wrists and shouting, "WHY won't you just listen to me?"

I was terrified inside but tried my best to hold it together, holding back the tears and trying not to breathe too fast and give the game away. Darren continued, "Now you've made me look like

I'm the one in the wrong when it was you. I just wanted you to listen but you wouldn't, you were stubborn. If you'd listened, then you would see that I'm just doing this because I love you so much and want to spend time with you."

I had figured out how to calm Darren down and it was to give up (feed him what he wanted) but I needed to look convincing so I had to believe that I was in the wrong; tears filled my eyes as I spoke apologetically and slowly, "I'm sorry, I know it was me but I was so tired and I wasn't thinking straight."

It was like a light switch flicked over in Darren, "See, I knew you knew it was you; don't worry I will forget about this, let's just get out of this rain and get home." We both headed home, drenched from head to toe and Darren held my hand lovingly. I held his back like a good girl.

* * *

Tears coursed down Rose's face; she was now shivering and her breath was visible every time she sobbed. Rose looked at the time on her iPhone, it had only been a minute but it felt like time had stopped still. Rose glazed over as she looked around. There was no one to be seen, not even any cars were in sight. She was sat in a slushy, muddy puddle but didn't move; she wouldn't care if she was cemented there like a statue. Rose sobbed more as she remembered the time when she realised she had lost control of what she could do for her future and make the choices she wanted to.

* * *

Once again I was asleep, in a deep dream remembering back to my ex-fiancé who kept saying he had forgiven me and taken me back after I realised my regret and was now with Darren. I often woke turning over and realising who I was sleeping next to and it wasn't my ex; then came the tears because this dream in particular was so vivid and life-like (even down to the smells and touch) that I truly believed it had happened. This night though, Darren had decided to wake me and wanted to talk about something not so urgent yet again.

"So were you going to tell me?" Darren was shaking me and repeating it over and over again. I knew what Darren was like after the last time he had behaved like this; the difference was that I was now seven months pregnant.

I managed to brush him off with a common and perfect pregnancy excuse, "I'm going to pee myself, hang on!!" and escaping his grip, I rushed to the bathroom and leapt onto the toilet. I had taken my iPhone with me; I remember having the blurry vision as I was still waking up; I made out the time and it was just 2am. There wasn't a lock on this bathroom door and it wasn't a surprise that Darren had followed me in moments later, even if I was in the middle of a long pee, but I knew what to do and ignored him.

"So were you going to tell me, then?" Darren started.

I began to rack my brain on how to manage the situation as I had gained that ability last time and at least it had calmed down even if I had swallowed my pride. "I don't know what you're talking about? But I am on the loo here," I replied thinking how was this going to go down. I was sat on the toilet waiting for him to leave so I could simply wipe up and pull my PJ bottoms up.

Darren didn't like the fact that I didn't know what he was talking about. "Don't act like you don't know when I know you do."

By this point, I realised he wasn't going to leave and started cleaning up and feeling very embarrassed that I couldn't have a little privacy. I washed my hands and headed to the door when Darren put his arm across so I couldn't pass. I didn't know how to react but he seemed more fired up and angry this time; it felt like a ticking time bomb all the time and you would never know when it would erupt. I felt it would be nice for it just to be done with, 'just hit me', I thought because then we could move on for another few weeks; I couldn't stand the way he made me nervous and on edge constantly.

I turned and Darren seemed to be distressed and not concentrating on me so I looked at my iPhone and thought, 'shall I chance letting someone know'? My heart was beginning to race and I started to get clammy; I didn't really know what this man was capable of because it wasn't the Darren I had first met. Everything seemed to have been fine since the last incident which I thought was a one-off (but clearly not).

Darren screamed in my face, "WELL?" He obviously thought I would know and I was racking my brain so hard to work out what on earth it was that was so bad.

"I'll give you a clue: you don't learn from your mistakes." Darren seemed to be getting more agitated because I simply had no idea.

"Did I not talk to you about something?" I replied thinking this could cover all bases but my voice gave away just how scared I was becoming; how was I meant to control the tremor?

Darren was beginning to think I was making fun and a mockery of him. "WHY are you doing this? YOU KNOW WHAT'S WRONG! Don't act stupid about it."

Darren was losing his temper more and was now face to face with me. I couldn't look him in the eye and had one hand in my pyjama pocket as I had my iPhone there. My iPhone never left my side, it is my security blanket (my best friend and worst enemy). I could even type on my iPhone without looking. I thought about my next move and what to do whilst Darren was screaming in my face. The teenage years of ignoring my parents whilst they told me off came into good use. I could hum a song in my head and still look like I was listening to them and taking it in. It seemed really childish but it worked and I had to do what got me through this.

I spoke, "Look, it's like I've said, it's really late and I'm not thinking straight, you know what I'm like when I first wake up," speaking softly to try and calm him down. "Let me just give my dad a ring 'cause he's good at putting me in my place and I've clearly upset you."

Darren erupted, "What, so you can put me down? I DONT THINK SO!" Darren started holding his head in his hands and pacing round near the door (my exit was now blocked), it was as if he was having a mental breakdown. I hadn't seen him behave like this before and was becoming increasingly worried as to what would happen next. He wasn't as irate the last time he had an issue with me. Darren began muttering to himself and trying to calm himself down; this completely freaked me out.

I thought I would be able to get my iPhone out as he seemed very distracted and not too concerned with me. I strategically and slowly put my hand in my pyjama pocket with my heart racing so fast that I thought Darren may be able to hear it. My hands were now shaking as I managed to get my iPhone into position in my palm but still in my pocket. I unlocked it and pressed the contacts app. This is where it became tricky, I had to get to my dad's phone number and ring it. I looked over my nose as I bent my hand to see the screen and started to tap, with much amazement; obviously my 24/7 iPhone use came through as it was ringing out to my dad.

It was like a lion catching its prey. Darren could hear my phone dialling out and punched straight to it. I had a hold of it so tightly it was like a fight for my life, gripping on, but Darren was too strong and he forced it out of my hand and then threw it on the cold tiled floor where it shattered into pieces. For a split second I thought that this would be it, he would calm down now he'd broken something but he swung for me with his fist so tight and face screaming with rage.

* * *

The thoughts became too much for Rose as she shook her head in her hands; tears broke through her fingers and she lightly bellowed as she felt a pain, her heart aching, her stomach churning and the flood of sickness overcame her. Then creeping around the corner she saw a familiar car appear and it mounted the kerb near Rose.

CHAPTER TWO

Rose's eyes were blurry and sore; she looked up at the car and a man was getting out of the scarlet red, top-of-the-range Alfa Romeo. Rose tried to focus her eyes but everything looked fuzzy and before she could see, she heard a deep voice, "What are you doing out here on your own?"

Instantly, Rose struggled and climbed up like she was intoxicated and then she collapsed into a handsome, jet-black-haired man's arms. It was Tim, a new business contact Rose had made just a few weeks ago. Rose had set up a business just 6 months ago and the thrust behind it was in fact, Darren. Darren had gotten so hot and heavy over her receptionist job that she had drastically cut the hours down to just 4 a week. Den didn't like having 'males' talk to her and Rose had only just a small circle of girlfriends left at work. In the end, it was easier for Rose to quit her job especially when she had come up with an idea that she could set up a business from her hobby; with this, she could work from home and have the business set up online (surely Darren couldn't argue with that). Rose had already become friends with a few mums in business and of course this was down her street because Rose was now a mum of two, Millie-Rose (an angelic 5-year-old) and Harrison (a cheeky, comedic 4-year-old).

Rose had met Tim at a networking breakfast where they did speed networking. This was meant to be 60 seconds about your business and how you could help the other networkers, but they both hit it off straight away and it was like they were speed-dating.

Tim had complimented her achievements in her new business in such a short time and Rose was so bashful she kept slowly pushing his arm and saying stop it. There was clearly chemistry between them and Rose was out of practice. Tim and Rose had instantly clicked and from then on they were emailing each other which soon turned into Facebook messaging and then developed into texting. Tim was such a gentleman, had offered to help if there was anything he could do and just to let him know. Rose was always too polite to ask of anyone and struggled along on her own. She didn't realise that Tim would become such a big help to her. Tim, at this point had no idea that his offer of help would stretch out to be personal and not just on a business level. He had fallen for her natural beauty with her big eyes and her intelligence and sense of humour.

Tim held Rose in his arms, "You're shivering and ice cold." Tim took off his tailor-made business jacket and placed it on Rose's shoulders and slowly started to guide her to his car. Rose continued to sob and couldn't believe the warmth of Tim's embrace would make her feel safe, as he helped her into his car. Rose didn't argue or dismiss his help, she allowed him to take care of her which was unusual for her.

Tim ran around the car and got in himself and turned the heat up high. "Let's get you to my place and we can try to sort this out."

Rose hadn't been to Tim's house before and she had no idea what to expect. Tim drove cautiously reckless which meant Rose had woken up a bit. As they approached Tim's house Rose was surprised, it was a lovely house which was the last house on the left in a cul-de-sac. A Victorian detached house with a garage, it was now late and Rose couldn't see all the detail in the nicely cut lawn.

Tim opened the passenger's door and helped Rose out of the car, clicked his key fob to lock it and then continued to assist Rose. Tim could feel that she was still cold and felt her tremble as her wet clothes and wet hair hit the frosty air.

Tim opened up the front door which led straight into the living room; there was a log file roaring with heat. Rose ran towards the fire and sat down in a heap. She could feel the flickers of the flames against her skin. Tim went to collect some blankets and a dressing gown which he brought to Rose and snuggled her up; he then continued to the kitchen where he put the kettle on. Once settled with a hot cup of tea, Rose began to tell Tim why she had gotten so upset and thought back to that moment Darren swung for her. Rose remembered it as if it had happened just moments ago.

* * *

Darren's clenched fist came with speed with all his anger behind it, but I captured it in slow motion. In fact, it's not the only time this had happened but yet I still couldn't move. I closed my eyes tight and thought I could imagine that this moment in time wasn't happening. There was a loud crashing noise followed by shattering glass and a moan from Darren, not what I was expecting. I was feeling scared to open my eyes and wondered why I wasn't hit; I thought this would be a good time to escape and opened my eyes and started to run but Darren grabbed me. There was blood everywhere, red running down his arm and beginning to cover me, it was all over the glass and bathroom floor.

"Oh my gosh!" I was concerned and threw myself at the towel rail to grab a hand towel and I quickly wrapped it 'round Darren's arm. Don't ask me why I helped him, he had even let go of my arm by this point but Darren wasn't saying anything and still looked rather pissed off.

"I'm going to ring for an ambulance." I now felt panicky and rushed off to get Darren sorted, the towel had become soaked in blood and he looked rather queasy. I could smell the iron and I became nauseous; this time Darren didn't argue back and accepted my assistance. Ringing 999 seemed to take forever; why is it when you actually need them, it rings for an eternity? An operator answered the phone and I spluttered everything out so fast that it didn't give the lady a chance to speak; I was nearly hyperventilating.

The lady operator managed to barge her way in and stopped me from continuing, "Ok, I've sent an ambulance but stay on the phone with me until it arrives..." she sounded like she had a peg gripped on to her nose but I didn't care and I let out a huge sigh of relief; I didn't want to be on my own in this situation any longer. I felt it would be nice to have someone with me in this moment of time, even if it was the emergency services. I had never felt so alone.

The operator continued, "Now, what happened?" I knew what she was doing, she was trying to diffuse the situation but also find out if I was okay, in a slightly parenting way. I hadn't thought they might ask what had actually happened to cause this and I suddenly felt there was a spotlight on me and that Darren could hear every word the operator and I were sharing. I couldn't risk telling her the real story, what if Darren was to hear?

And so I replied, "Well, you see it was all my fault." I didn't sound convincing at all. "We had an argument and I let it go too far."

The operator said, "Do you need the police to come over?" By that time, I was now uncontrollably crying.

"All you have to do is say *yes* or *no* to me," the operator was trying to reassure me. I couldn't believe it. I managed to pronounce the word 'yes' very quietly and nervously but I thought I would have safety soon. The operator had started to calm me down and it was simply because someone was listening to me; no one had done that before, but this was the first time I had even recognised something was wrong and that I needed help.

"The ambulance will be there any moment now, so don't worry." Darren had left me alone and he was sat on the tiled floor of the bathroom still holding his arm mumbling something about needing a fag. Suddenly there were three loud thuds on the door; they had arrived. I let out a huge sigh as I had never felt so relieved in all my life. It seemed like hours had passed by; the ambulance crew seemed friendly towards me and they came in to the house and began their job. By the time the police had arrived, they were taking large pieces of glass out of Darren's arm. The ambulance crew were not happy with Darren and made no eye contact. I remember being worried that they had been told I had asked for the police and that Darren might pick up on it being 'my fault'.

I went and sat in the front room and left the ambulance crew to do their work. I was sobbing and staring into space; I could only see my life through tunnel vision and it was bleak. The police snapped me out of it and I was apologetic, I couldn't bear the thought that they might have been thinking I was losing the plot. Again, the police were polite towards me offering reassurance; they were stern with Darren and I only imagined that this would come to bite me bitterly on my bum for years to come.

That night Darren received a verbal warning and the notes were written up on the log; they gave me the log number and a small leaflet away from Darren's sight. I knew exactly what the leaflet was going to say but I wasn't going through that, couples have arguments like this all the time, right? The police told him to buck up his ideas as I was just 5 months pregnant and it's not about my health but the baby's health too.

"Let's not add any stress onto her," the police officer told Darren which looked like she was trying to drill the words into his skull.

I remember thinking, 'stop it, you're only going to make it worse'. How could I tell them this without Darren hearing: I wished I had telepathic powers.

* * *

Rose found herself sobbing again but she wasn't as distraught; Tim was there and he held her in his arms. He was so warm and Rose's tears were welcome on his shoulder. Tim stroked her hair and cradled her in his strong arms; the firelight glistened on his jet black hair. Rose couldn't bear it, questions kept filling her head. Why did she think this was normal for couples? Why couldn't she have left then? Why didn't she read the stupid leaflet? Why couldn't she see the signs? Why would no one shake her so she would see the true colours that were so obvious?

There was something about Tim that was different, not only had he listened to Rose but he valued her and Rose hadn't felt like this for a very long time. She had set herself a rule to remain single for a minimum of five years because she didn't want her or her children to get hurt or confused. This would enable her to concentrate on her children and her business. However, reality didn't seem to be working out like this. Rose was falling for Tim. She loved the feeling of someone caring for her; it had only highlighted just how lonely she was. Rose was afraid of getting stuck in another bad situation and she was cautious of everyone. Naturally, she had lost trust in everyone but herself. Tim was becoming someone very special, very fast and for some reason, Rose didn't feel scared.

Tim seemed to have a calming effect on Rose but he only knew what she had told him and he felt so much worry for her and a natural urge to help. Tim had witnessed just how much stress and strain this was taking on Rose, even to the extent of her physically vomiting after every meal and being so overwhelmed with migraines that she would pass out.

Rose's two children were the reason she was still in this situation. Darren had threatened her and used Millie-Rose and Harrison as weapons so much that it was safer to stay put. Countless times Darren had said he would get custody of the children and tell the court how Rose had severe bipolar disorder (which wasn't true). Rose was so scared of losing them that she went to the doctors to check if she had the disorder. It was important for Rose that her mind was at rest as she had started to believe what Darren was saying and a course of elimination was how Rose now worked.

Rose kept thinking about her children; Millie-Rose was a beautiful big-blued-eyed girl full of personality and very sociable and Harrison was a very cheeky chap who loved to trick and tease anyone. Tim could see that these two children were more than just a reason, they were Rose's way of surviving for the last 6 years of her life.

Tim went to make her a fresh hot cup of tea; Rose had warmed up a little and was feeling better now she had talked it through with someone. Rose started to observe where she was; Tim's home was stunning. It had traditional aspects with modern art and technology; she thought to herself that his business must be doing him well but why would he have the time for her? She couldn't see any family photos around the room or even any photos of him. Rose thought she may find some clues to be able to start a conversation. When Tim returned, Rose's face lit up, she had never been treated like this by a man.

"Thank you so much, you don't know how much it means," she began to speak and hugged her cup of tea with her hands.

Tim sat on his cream leather sofa near Rose and cautiously asked, "Where are your family? Do they know what's going on?"

"They are in technically in Liverpool but on the outskirts. I moved to York for university and basically met Darren and ended up staying here; I've always wanted to go back. Anyway, I don't speak to them that much and I haven't been back for over two years now."

Rose's face washed with desperation and Tim thought it was best to change the tone and lighten things up. "Ok, come on tell me what's your favourite food?"

Rose smiled and replied, "Mexican."

"How about I take you out for Mexican on Saturday night?"

Tim casually asked.

"You already know my answer," Rose spoke with a huge grin and had a giddy feeling coming over her; she didn't care how she was going to sort it with Darren but she was going to go and enjoy herself.

A couple of hours had gone and it was past midnight when Tim asked a nervous question, "So... what do you want to do from here? Shall I take you home now?" Rose knew she couldn't stay with him forever and did have to be back for the children in the morning as Darren was in work. It was very rare for her to leave the children and this was the first time away from them on a night. Rose was over-protective of Millie-Rose and Harrison and only left them with the nursery. Darren had given her no choice as he was impatient; Rose treated it as if she was a single mum and did everything that involved the children.

Rose instantly started to be apologetic and thought how selfish she must have seemed. "Of course, I'm so sorry, I've taken up so much of your time already and I can see you're a busy man." Rose suddenly felt a huge wash of guilt in her gut.

Tim raised one eyebrow, knelt down to her eye level and looked at her straight in the eyes and said firmly, "First of all you don't need to thank me and second of all I have already said I will help you and I mean that. I don't offer help lightly."

Rose tried to interrupt but Tim put his pointed finger to her lips and said to her, "Please listen to me: you are welcome to stay here and I don't just mean tonight but if you need to come and stay for a few weeks or months, even if it's to have a break from him. I don't have a big family and I get pretty lonely which I'm guessing you know how that feels? I've got to be honest, I've never done this before but there's something about you that makes me want to help and I am concerned about you. You have my personal number and you never have to worry about what I'm doing, just ring."

Rose couldn't believe what she was hearing and kept feeling that she didn't want to go back at all; it felt nice to feel cared for.

Tim continued, "Can I ask you something?" Rose nodded at him, wondering what he was going to ask. "What on earth were you doing with someone like him? I mean I can tell just from meeting you on a couple of occasions that you're not stupid!"

Rose let out a sigh and actually wondered just how she was

going to answer that question.

"I can't say I was stupid and I can't say I was clever because honestly I didn't expect to get into this situation, I don't really know how it's gone on this far without me realising exactly what was happening and to be honest I don't see myself as a victim – I just see fault and blame on my part for not getting out sooner. But the thing is Tim, I was scared! In the end HE actually ended the relationship with me and it was all because I found out about him sleeping with someone else. He blamed me for finding out! This was only a few months ago and I hadn't long met you after. I know when I met him he used to say such wonderful things about me; he used to spoil me, take me shopping, wine and dine me and honestly you wouldn't think anything of it. It didn't take me long to realise I had made the wrong decision and by that time I was stuck away from my family with my name on a rental agreement. How was I supposed to get out?"

Tim was watching Rose struggle to answer the question and offered to help. "I think you will find I can understand but I won't until I live it with you. I wanted to ask because I want to be able to make sure that you know that you won't see that behaviour and that pattern happen in me. Ok, I may spoil you and wine and dine you but I don't plan to stop that and I don't plan to isolate you – in fact I want the opposite of that."

Rose was hanging on every single word and was welling up. Tim kissed the top of her forehead. Rose didn't know what to say and with water-filled eyes, she was desperately trying not to let a single tear drop.

She took a risk by leaning towards Tim for a kiss. Rose felt like the kiss wasn't going to be received as she was sat still with her lips pursed waiting, her palms were becoming hot and she was feeling nervous until at last, she felt Tim's lips slowly kiss her in return. His hands ran through her hair as he held her head and brought her closer to him. Rose was overcome with pins and needles straight to her tummy which fluttered with butterflies which weren't at all familiar. Rose's heart was now racing and she knew Tim wasn't a quivering wreck like her but a handsome man that had chosen her.

Rose and Tim were kissing for at least ten minutes and the intensity was building. Tim managed to get up onto one knee and held out his hand, expecting Rose to take it. Rose had a moment's pause and slowly reached to place her soft hand in his firm one; he helped her up and walked over to the bottom of the stairs. Rose was feeling more and more nervous and light-headed; she had only slept with Darren and one other and didn't feel one bit confident. Tim allowed Rose to go by his side up the stairs; he kept hold of her hand and placed the other just above her bottom.

Rose was so hot that she needed to get some cool air; Tim on the other hand showed no nerves but complete sexiness. They had reached the top of the stairs and Tim was steering her around the corner and to the 4th and last room. Tim leant over her to open the door and he could feel Rose's body heat and could hear her heart thumping hard.

CHAPTER THREE

The sun filtered through a small break in the beige curtains onto Rose's face. Rose woke with a wince and a smile; she was thinking about last night and how Tim made her feel.

Rose rolled over and let out a scream. "Ahhhhh, what do you think you're doing?" Darren was there staring back at her just like he had been watching her all night.

"It's my bed too you know, I can't sleep on the sofa any longer," and he blew his cigarette smoke into her face. Rose was already irritated and out of patience with him.

"I've told you to set up a single bed in the dining room or something, you can't just do this!"

The response she received was, "Well, I have and now I'm going to get ready for work," Darren said like a young teenager with attitude.

When Darren had finally gone to work and Rose had got her two munchkins up, she brewed up a hot mug of tea. This was Rose's morning routine and would follow with another 15 cups of tea before the day was out. Millie-Rose was playing with her kitchen and making her mummy and Harrison her own version of tea with her felt teabags. Harrison was playing with his car walker and was making his way over to Millie-Rose to bash into her feet as he loved to do. Rose sat down and snuggled into her warm leather sofa and hugged her mug of tea. She watched her two children with a smile on her face and couldn't imagine life without them. Rose had always wanted to be a mum since she was 10 years old; it was a huge life aspiration for her and she always wanted to get it 'right' and be the best she could be.

Millie-Rose handed Rose a mini pretend cup of tea and smiled gleefully. She was pleasantly happy and gave her mummy a long-lasting hug. She often overly-hugged her mummy. They had this true mummy and daughter unbreakable bond and Rose valued this as she felt it was missing from her own life. Harrison bashed his way through his toys and joined in by hugging Rose's leg as he couldn't quite reach over his car walker. They all said loudly together, 'awwwww' and giggled.

Rose was quickly overcome with emotion and her eyes were filling up with tears. She couldn't conceal them; she knew her children could have a better life if Darren and her finally separated. Rose couldn't bear the atmosphere that she knew the children would easily be picking up on, especially as Darren had become even more impatient since they officially separated three months prior.

Three months under the same roof was already becoming too much and Rose hated the children being put in the middle like this. For too long, Rose had held onto the fact she didn't want a broken family like her own parents and it end in divorce; it wasn't going to work out and it wasn't a healthy example of a relationship to the children; it was damaging. Thinking about all those times Darren hurt her, she thought again back to when she was pregnant with Millie-Rose.

* * *

It had just been a month since the police and ambulance crew were around at our house. Darren was left with big deep scars all down his arm and even some little scars on his face; this hadn't bothered him. On this particular day I had planned to meet my older sister Scarlett in Leeds, somewhere a bit different where we hadn't been before. I had planned to get on the train and have a shopping day with her which I hadn't done since I was around thirteen. I didn't get on too well with my mum so I had looked up to Scarlett most of my life; we could be best friends and worst enemies but Scarlett still was the perfect big sister anyone could ask for. We were also going to meet to discuss some medical history in the family, obviously I was already eight months' pregnant and that's something that should have been discussed a lot earlier in the pregnancy. I started to get ready for my day out with my big sis; I was looking forward to it as if it was the most important day in the world but soon realised the reason why.

I was running from the bathroom to the bedroom and rushing around like women do, shower done, hair done, matching clothes done, makeup done. Darren lay in bed having a smoke and a mug of coffee watching me with a slight squint. I had felt the presence of his eyes on me all morning and knew what he was doing but I ignored it; I would be out of the house soon enough and I would have a bit of freedom.

"You look nice." Darren had finally decided to speak and it was literally just as I was putting on my shoes. "Aww, thank you," I said, feeling slightly anxious.

"So, why did Scarlett want to meet you without me?" There was a pause, I had no idea how to respond. "Or was it your idea?" I had started to stutter as I could already foretell where this was going.

"Oh, it was her idea; I think it's nice as we haven't met up in so long. It's nothing to do with not wanting you there, in fact I think we're planning another time to meet with you which will be nice, won't it?" Darren was hard in thought and I could tell he was trying to work out if I was lying; he thought he could read me like a book but he couldn't be any more wrong.

"Oh right, I just think it's odd that's all," he took a drag from his smoke and slowly exhaled and there was another pause.

"Well, I better be getting off, I don't want to miss my train." I spoke with more caution than haste whilst keeping my head down as I spoke. The switch had been flicked in Darren once again; it seemed to be a lot more sensitive these days and I didn't have to do much to trigger it. I even tried to avoid it but nothing I did was right and I could correct my 'mistakes' over and over again but had no joy.

"You're going to be talking about me, aren't you?" his voice started to get louder. "Why am I having to sit here all day why you plot and back chat ME?" Darren was beginning to wind himself up. I didn't know what to do so I cowered.

"You know that's not true, I love you, we're just talking about the medical stuff." Darren had been given some ammunition.

"SO DONT YOU THINK THAT I SHOULD BE THERE? It is my baby too! Unless there's something you have to tell me."

I knew exactly what Darren was going to say and I couldn't believe that Darren was trying to imply it and I nearly laughed, I had never left his side; I never went out with friends so what possible time could that give me to have sex with anyone else, never mind an affair. I thought a firm response would be good.

"Well, that's not possible and I'm with you and love you; what reason would I have to do that? I'm just going to see my sister and have lunch and do some shopping. It's completely harmless." The guilt trip came next; I had become very familiar with the pattern.

"If you LOVED me, I would be coming with you." Suddenly, Darren threw his half-drunk mug of coffee at me. I had not expected this and it smashed against the wall just an inch from my face; a couple of little shards sliced the left side of my face, right near my eye. I remember holding my face with one hand and there was a little blood. I looked down and saw that the mug was one of mine that my father had given to me when I was a teenager. It read 'Daddy's little girl forever' on it. I felt like I was going to cry, but I managed to overcome the emotion and speak.

"Why are you doing this? I've said I love you. That was my mug you've broken and it meant something to me."

Darren was quick to answer; he was always fast and never left anyone room for thought. That's why it was so easy to turn it on me all the time. "Well, you shouldn't have given me a reason. If you go on your own, then don't come back."

I felt like I was being locked up in a prison cell and he was throwing away the key; the happy day that was planned was now interfered with and I would have to watch what I said for the rest of the day. I had become used to minding my body language as any slight glance or smirk or incorrect comment or even a joke could set Darren off. I was still clumsy but I was getting better at being an emotionless robot lately. I was blunt with my words again.

"The train goes in 25 minutes so we have to leave in 5 minutes," and I left the room to go downstairs and wait for Darren as clearly he was planning to bombard my shopping trip with my sister. It was pointless because he would only be complaining that he had a boring day looking around the shops. Nevertheless, I waited for him and sure enough he came down and he led the way out the door as if he was my bodyguard. I wasn't able to go anywhere without him more than a couple of meters away from me whenever I was out in public. We walked to the train station in pure silence, I felt nothing but resentfulness and I wanted to scream; thank goodness I had learnt how to put a smile on my face.

* * *

Rose often daydreamed, not only of deep flashbacks but also of her future. It used to be positive with thoughts of having a happy little family and her own home. Rose was full of morals and she wanted to prove that marriages don't always end in divorce and was adamant whomever she was to marry that it would be forever – no going back. Rose's dreams had changed a lot, especially in the latter months; she now imagined herself homeless, poor, and on benefits for the rest of her life. She was afraid her children would follow the pattern of Darren's family: drug abuse, violence and involvement with the police. Rose could see life was spiralling out of control and that the mould was starting to set.

She had been brought up in a working class home and saw her mum and dad work hard for their detached house in a cute village outside of Liverpool. Rose believed in the same concept – work hard and achieve your goals because you won't get anywhere if you don't. The dream had slipped over the years she was with Darren but after setting up her business and finding an ounce of determination for herself, Rose had started to build her confidence again. Connections she made had complimented her and it had started to fill the gap that was missing; she had started to believe she could be successful. Darren thought that she would fail right from the beginning and made sure Rose was fully aware of this but Rose believed in filling your life with positive people who helped you and encouraged you. This would keep her fighting for a better life.

Rose had begun to focus her mind and she managed to start having little positive moments that were like water dropping into a still lake. Even though Rose had been told constantly it was a waste of time and wasn't bringing in any money, she still strived to carry on. It also meant she had an excuse to be in a different room or not talk to him as she sat in the dining room building her business on an evening. It was a perfect resolution at the time for the problem that was facing her every minute of each day. Rose kept telling herself what she had learnt through research, 'it takes three years to start making a profit on a business and to begin to pay yourself'. Rose even started to talk positive to herself in the mirror which was really difficult to begin with. This was her nest-egg and she was going to see it through; she wanted her children to see how hard-working she was and to be able to provide for them.

Rose wanted to get out of the housing-trust house she lived in, even though others told her there was nothing wrong with this and her Auntie Lucy had told her, "it doesn't matter where your house is as long as you make it a home. If you can step in through the front door and feel that homeliness, then that's all that matters."

Rose did hold onto this and made the house feel warm and middle class on the inside but it still wasn't enough and didn't take away from the fact that the area wasn't good for the children. There were often disturbances down the street and Rose didn't like Millie-Rose and Harrison going out in the back garden in the summer. The neighbour's mum would be swearing at her children and every other word would be an inappropriate word. Darren had never seemed to mind because his family lived on the same street and it was like he was immune to the language and foul behaviour.

Millie-Rose had started making play dinner for Harrison and Rose now; Rose loved to feed their imaginations and play along. How easy life seemed for children. Sugar-coated is an understatement to the reality of how life works. Rose loved to be in a carefree bubble with them. It was easy for Rose as she had younger cousins she used to look after as well as the amateur dramatics she used to take part in. The most important thing right now was to make plastic sweetcorn in a pan and pretend it was warm and yummy. Millie-Rose and Harrison would giggle uncontrollably when Rose nibbled her plastic sweetcorn, like in the cartoons.

Rose would do anything for her children and this was one of the thousand reasons to stay and suffer in this situation. There seemed only a hundred reasons to leave. Included in the hundred reasons to leave would be for Rose's health and sanity, to see her family more and regain friendships, to be independent and not feel like she was suffocated. But these were over-shadowed with the thousand reasons she had convinced herself of. She would be homeless with her children, there would be no money and she was already in debt. Darren and his family would come after her, she would have to leave all of her possessions, and it might mean closing the business she had started to build.

Fears of making the wrong choice for her children, fears that she couldn't cope, were all niggling at her conscious. Rose had baggage and would be alone; Rose wasn't worth the trouble. Most of the reasons had been drummed into her by Darren, and he had tied her up in knots financially. There were too many consequences of leaving; staying seemed like the safest option especially as Rose was already immune to Darren's ways. It was only recently that she had started to feel what happiness was like and the urge to change the way her life was going. Could she break free? Rose remembered a time that she thought she could.

CHAPTER FOUR

I was downstairs looking after Millie-Rose when she was just over 18 months old; she loved to play in her ball pit and her hair had grown enough to be able to French-plait it. My auntie had always French-plaited my hair and I used to love getting it done and so I found it very heart-warming to do Millie-Rose's.

I had my iPhone 3 at the time and loved how I used Safari to sign into Darren's Facebook account; yes, I didn't trust him and yes, I was insecure. He had done a good job at making me feel this way. Den had been acting weirdly over the last few weeks and I had forgotten I could check his Facebook and for some reason it came to me for no particular reason.

It was a normal sunny morning and Millie-Rose was playing innocently and Harrison was kicking away in my tummy and making me feel queasy. I wasn't prepared for what I was about to read. I was just about to crack open the pickled onion jar with the bar of marzipan in my hands to satisfy my peculiar cravings, when I started to look through his messages and I could see the usual male friends but my eyes were directed to a girl I had never met or heard of before. I clicked into the messages and went onto her profile.

'Claire Thornby' had a profile picture showing off her very generous cleavage and her lovely slim figure and I knew instantly that I would have to be cautious. I clicked back into the messages and scrolled up – they had been chatting a lot by the looks of the feed. I didn't need to read much because when I read the lines, 'I had fun last night' ... 'I loved you in that bikini, you looked amazing' and her replies, 'You really had your way with me' ... 'when are we meeting up again'. I knew exactly what he had done; he had cheated on me and my assumption was that this wasn't the first time.

I suddenly felt so angry and frustrated and I couldn't understand why he would do this. He constantly went on and on about me not being able to go out alone because he was worried other men would come onto me and I wouldn't say no, when really it was him worried that he had gotten away with it and he thought maybe I had too! I was so angry because he had treated me like a stereotypical 1950s housewife and I obliged because I thought he has an issue that he didn't know how to control. I felt completely stupid, humiliated, embarrassed and ashamed because what would my family and friends think? Why should I be subjected to feeling like this when it should be him feeling guilty and ashamed with himself but I knew that if it came out, he wouldn't. He was care-free and if he did care, then he had a great way of hiding it. I was thinking about everyone else's reaction and what it would mean but I hadn't thought of just how much it would affect me.

And before I knew it, I felt hot, cold, shaky, angry, happy, distraught and overwhelmed. I was alone in this and I was expecting our second child.

I got Millie-Rose ready and headed out for the day; I couldn't be in the same house as him and he didn't know that I had found this out. I didn't know how I was going to drop this in the conversation! I was trying not to have a panic attack and thankfully Millie-Rose was a great distraction and always kept me focused on something else. I hurried off down the road in the green Ford Fiesta with Millie-Rose singing to herself happily. It wasn't long before I had to pull over to be sick and I thought to myself that it was a good job I hadn't eaten those pickled onions. I got back in the car and had to get away.

I decided to park up not far away from the city centre of York and walk in. I had a gentle walk with Millie-Rose in her pushchair and she soon wanted to stop and enjoy one of her favourite things with Mummy and that was going to Costa and getting a coffee. OK, Millie-Rose had a juice but I would always treat her by sharing my chocolate tiffin.

Millie-Rose was in her pushchair making a huge mess out of a tiny bit of this treat and I just wanted to break down in tears. I felt like a failure and I felt this made me a bad parent but it wasn't my fault! I knew what my answer would have been before meeting Darren and the type of person I was. I wouldn't have taken any of this shit and would've left him straight away. The truth was, how on earth was I going to leave him without it being difficult; where was I going to go? How would I cope when I was pregnant, how could I cope financially? I already knew at this point in the relationship that I was trapped in a corner and there seemed to be no way out. If there was, it certainly wasn't clear and it would mean going through a lot of stress and by stress I don't mean the usual stresses of a break-up but fear of what he might do as a result of a break-up.

Millie-Rose was now showing me her creative personality, and was drawing pictures in her chocolate-spit mess on the side of the table. All the while, I was having an internal battle. Could I let this go over my head? Could I pretend I didn't know? Could I carry on? But the answer to each question was a big fat 'no'. Even an actor couldn't do that. By now I was even plotting a dramatic solution in my head and getting my hair died and chopped off so I could escape and be unrecognisable, rush off and start my new happy life; that would be nice but I knew I wouldn't get far before he'd track me down. There were so many reasons as to why I had to stay; it was completely depressing.

I read over some of the messages again and I felt so angry and I felt like this because actually it was like I was suffering for no reason; he would put me through crazy crap and even accused me of having an affair, God knows how many times, when in fact it was him playing away behind my back. I knew that if I mentioned this to him that it would somehow be turned around and brought back to me as my fault and I was the reason for his actions. I was just getting myself upset again and so I used up a ridiculous amount of wipes on Millie-Rose and went back out for another walk. I headed down the shambles, that little Diagon Alley style path (like Harry Potter) of crooked slanting houses and they always cheered me up. I loved to see the tourists taking photos of themselves down it and it has a presence of feeling magical.

I had been walking with Millie-Rose for a good couple of hours when Darren texted me to ask where I was and I didn't answer. I didn't know how to and my silence spoke the words to him. Millie-Rose was nagging for a drink. I popped into the nearest newsagents and got her a black currant fruit shoot and on the way to the checkout I saw some paracetamol on the shelf so I picked up a couple of packets as I had a stinking headache. The checkout girl looked very bored and almost like a zombie with her baseball cap on and head to one side. 'Next please', she called out like a drone without even glancing my way. I went over and paid for my few little bits and snuck in a cheeky chocolate bar before she ran off the total to me. Millie-Rose and I continued to have a walk around and we enjoyed the sun, nipped for a quick swing in the park and looked at the children's selection of DVDs in an entertainment shop. To be honest, I didn't want to go home at all; I wanted to ride away and find happiness with my little girl and baby.

We worked our way back to the car and the old banger was waiting for us. I always looked at Emerald and thought she had done us well and seemed to have a personality; she had squeaky wiper blades and a light that would always blow every few months (which was highly inconvenient).

We got settled in the car and I had my light shopping on the passenger seat. I scoffed the chocolate bar as I had started to snivel once again; hiding my tears was hard when you have a beautiful girl smiling at you in the rear view mirror. Millie-Rose drank all her fruit shoot and was now wanting something else to eat. I hunted through the shopping bag and found some baby crisps and handed them to Millie who was screeching with excitement to get them. I saw the paracetamol out of the corner of my eye and paused. I then hurriedly opened both packets and one by one in no time at all, I swallowed all of the tablets. I don't know what I was thinking; no, I did. I could end this misery for good, I could no longer be under his control, I could be free and I felt happy about it.

I sat in the car waiting, thinking it would happen instantly, thinking I wouldn't have time to second guess my decision. I looked back at my beautiful Millie-Rose and I burst into tears. What about her, I thought? What life would I be leaving for her? She wouldn't get the upbringing I would want for her and she deserved the best. Millie-Rose started to ask me, "Why you cry, Mummy? It ok, Mummy. Love you."

I had never felt so guilty and so trapped, I couldn't even end this if I wanted to. I couldn't end my own life. I didn't even have control over that. I needed to stay to make sure Millie-Rose was protected and to make sure she had the best of a bad situation –

no, a diabolically and desperately bad situation. I couldn't control my floods of tears and I kept thinking about her future and what it would be like without me. I kept thinking about what she would become; I felt like a bad mother having brought her into this life we were living.

I recognised that I needed to get the drugs out of my system and fast. It didn't matter that I was parked on a busy street near the city centre, it didn't matter what I had to do! I started to jam my fingers down my throat, out of Millie-Rose's sight, and opened the car door... it didn't take long to do. I managed to make myself sick but it was a painful acid bile as all I had eaten was a chocolate bar. I couldn't chance it and kept making myself sick until there was nothing left; what about the baby, I thought? I'm not a cruel and horrible person. Gosh how stupid I felt and how immature it was to do something like this. My sick was splattered by the side of the car all over the pavement. There were no passers-by but even if there had been, I wouldn't have cared.

After just five minutes of emptying myself, I went around to Millie-Rose's side of the car, opened the door and hugged her and gave her a kiss and said, "I love you so much you know, I'm never going to leave you, ever."

I made her that promise there and then. It made me realise that I needed to train myself not to be bothered by Darren because I couldn't get into this state again. There was no way I would ever leave my Millie-Rose in this mess. I thought I would feel resentful of her but I didn't; she in fact was giving me the strength to carry on and the focus I needed to train myself.

* * *

Rose often couldn't enjoy time with her children with the pressure and strain, not to mention the bad atmosphere within the household. She couldn't focus and kept thinking about how she had independently cared for the children over the years. When Darren lost his temper through his lack of patience, then it wouldn't be Rose who it would affect, he would take it out on the children. Rose couldn't help but think about how Darren's controlling behaviour had started to migrate onto the children.

* * *

It was a nice, mild midweek day and Harrison was just a few months old. I loved to breastfeed and believed it was best for my children. Darren always had an issue with it and made it extremely difficult for me to feel comfortable and relax, even if we were at home.

Darren would make remarks like, "It would be nice to feed my son too, you know, I don't feel like I even contribute."

I was feeding Harrison at the time and Millie-Rose needed to go to the toilet as she was now successfully potty-trained. I asked politely, "Darren, could you take Millie-Rose to the toilet please? I shouldn't be too long with Harrison but it would help a lot."

Darren responded with that stare and I knew it meant I was on thin ground already because I hadn't got round to hoovering or doing any of the household chores. Millie-Rose went up and took her time on the toilet and was singing away. I remember hearing Darren's heavy sighs through the ceiling. It wasn't as if I had disturbed him in the middle of an important task, he had just been sat with his phone like he usually does.

God only knew what happened next; it must have been that Millie-Rose had started to mess about but Darren came stomping down the stairs with Millie-Rose in a rugby hold position. She was screaming and kicking and he then slammed her down on the bottom step (which was the naughty step). I cringed as I heard the dull, hard thud and knew it would have hurt her bottom. I could see he had slammed her down from waist height. Darren came back into the living room and slammed the door hard so Millie-Rose was left in the pitch black hallway as there were no windows providing any light.

I had to ask, even though I was concerned about what he may do to me. I needed to know and do what mothers do best and protect. "What was she doing?" I asked with a nervous giggle.

Darren responded with a slight snap, "Just the usual, using too much toilet roll."

I thought this was an inadequate reason to react the way he had and felt sorry for Millie-Rose. I defended her, "Kids are kids, I guess?"

Darren gave me that stare again and I knew I was starting to push my luck, however I struggled up as I was still feeding Harrison. I had become a master at walking around and doing basic tasks whilst still breastfeeding Harrison (yes, I was rather proud of this but I also had no option).

I went to see Millie-Rose who had a very red bum and would definitely bruise. Millie-Rose was clearly in distress and pain and I comforted her and couldn't care less if Darren was going to punish me for it. I held Millie-Rose in my arms and I wanted to tell her that I was going to take her away and keep her safe, I wanted to tell her she would be ok. I wanted to tell her that no matter what happens she will be ok but I couldn't because I couldn't be sure and I couldn't break a promise to her. I knew that I needed to do whatever it took to protect her no matter what it cost me. I stroked her hair and she cuddled into my bosom, light tears started to fill my eyes and gently glide down my face; I had never loved as much as the love I felt for Millie-Rose and Harrison.

I could hear Darren clanging the teaspoon into his mug, banging the cupboard doors in the kitchen and muttering to himself with the occasional grunt. In a way I laughed at this, how pathetic. Millie-Rose is just a little girl and he is letting her get the better over him, over the toilet!

If that wasn't enough, already that night I had accidentally slept through Harrison crying for his next feed at around 3am. Normally I would wake as I was in-tune like a digital radio tuned into one radio station: the parent channel. I woke up to the warning cry that Harrison was giving, that horrible cry that babies give when there is really something wrong.

I ran into Harrison's room unsure of what was going on or what was wrong with him. Adrenalin was pumping through me. When I stumbled into his room, I couldn't believe what I saw.

Darren was banging his fists onto the cot mattress either side of Harrison and shouting in his face, "Shut up you f**king cock, what do you want? I'm trying to sleep!"

I pushed Darren out of the way and took Harrison into my arms immediately and started to cradle him to calm down his crying. I whispered to him, "It's OK, Mummy is here now, I need to wake up faster for you."

I remember feeling a loss for my children that they didn't really have a dad and had a bully living with them instead. I knew then that I better be even more in-tune; a drop of a pin and I would need to respond quickly. I was like a single parent; I was forced to be this way to protect my children. I didn't mind because they are my world and they were the reason I kept living each day. I realised from this moment that it was no longer me that was getting hurt but the children were now being dragged into it. I remember feeling in that moment that all respect and any feelings I used to have for Darren of love and friendship, were now gone.

* * *

Thinking back always made Rose focus on getting out as soon as she could because her children deserved to be loved the right way and to grow up in a healthy relationship. Rose feared that they would think the relationship between their mum and dad was normal, but it was far from it. Rose feared that they would then look at Darren's family and see the dead-end city of relationships that they lived in. Rose rolled her eyes back as she cuddled Millie-Rose more and remembered back to before Millie-Rose and Harrison were born.

* * *

I was over at Darren's mum's house and we got on surprisingly well; to be honest I got on with any of my boyfriend's mothers in the past and I didn't see why we needed to have any friction because I was a well-educated young woman with a lot of potential and I was hard-working for it. We were chatting over a cup of tea with 'Come Dine With Me' on in the background. I was rather addicted to this show when it first came out and had all the time in the world to try out different recipes. I was expecting my first bundle of joy and I believed it to be important for me to be involved with Darren's family; it was a big one at that.

Darren's mum was called Joan and she was often referred to as Jo. She was a short lady with bleached blonde hair, it was almost white. Darren was doing some of the decorating over at our place ready for the arrival of our bundle of joy and his sister, Katie, had offered to help despite her being just 13 at the time. Nevertheless, I enjoyed Joan's company and we talked about something or nothing, that's what we did best. After a couple of hours, I had become tired and decided to walk home which was just a street across. Katie had gone by now and Darren was finishing up the room. I decided to pop my feet up and I stuck the TV on and watched complete rubbish; it was in no time I fell asleep.

It wasn't until a few days later when Darren was taking me out for a meal that I discovered a locket out of my jewellery box wasn't in its rightful place. "Darren…. Darren…" I was trying to get him to hear me despite him being downstairs and with the TV on blaring away. "DARREN!" Urgh that was it, I marched down the stairs in irritation that he hadn't heard me and to be honest I was a grumpy, hormonal pregnant woman, so I did have some leeway. I barged the living-room door open and was out of breath… "Darren…" I tried to catch my breath.

Darren paused the Sky TV as if it was an inconvenience that I had even addressed him.

"My locket isn't there…have you seen it?"

"Why would I have seen it? You know what you're like at misplacing things. It's probably somewhere else."

I was getting even more grumpier as I wanted some help in finding it. "Well, can you help me look for it?!" And with great annoyance to him he started hunting round the place with me with no results.

Days passed and it didn't come up and to be honest I am one for misplacing things but not something as precious as this locket; it was my aunt's and she had passed away a few years ago and I was so close to her. It was expensive and I kept it safe. In the end I knew it. I knew what had happened.

This miserable day had come along and Darren was on the phone to his mum; Katie had been taken down to the police station for theft. I couldn't believe it and the penny dropped. How on earth was I going to talk to Darren about this? As soon as Darren got off the phone, I went for it, simply because I had to.

"Darren, I overheard a bit of that…is everything all right?"

He didn't hesitate either, "Not really, bloody Katie again upsetting mum because of her immature decisions; she's down the police station because the local shop caught her stealing from them."

I was concerned for his mum, as I did get on with Joan. "Oh, no…is your mum ok?"

"She will be; she's used to this really but it doesn't stop me from being annoyed."

"I know now is not the best time, but I think I need to say it…I think Katie took the locket."

Darren shifted a look my way and was about to interrupt.

"BECAUSE...'cause she was over that day helping you and then my locket goes missing!"

Darren wasn't even angry at me, it was weird. He replied, "Oh, well I was going to talk to you about that."

I didn't know what to think. "Talk to me about what?"

Darren then tried to smooth me up with compliments. "Well, you know you're always getting on with my mum, you're amazing like that; you know I am really lucky to have you because my family is a mess and you accept them for who they are." I just looked at him with a blank expression. "My mum needed some money and Katie was looking through your jewellery box and I was saying it was worth something."

"NOT THAT IT MEANS SOMETHING TO ME? HOW DARE YOU LET HER LOOK THROUGH MY THINGS!" I was starting to panic, starting to gasp and struggle to breathe. I couldn't explain the anger, the upset, the disappointment and the betrayal I felt. I tried to calm down. "And you just LET her take it?"

Darren then spoke up, "No, no, no...I wasn't there, she took it, but she did tell me a few days later when I mentioned you'd lost it."

I was sweating, I was that hot with rage; no care, no feelings, no sympathy, no empathy, no nothing! "So why didn't you tell me????" and Darren replied, "Because I didn't want you to change your opinion of my family."

Use my good will against me and then say my good will isn't good enough! I took myself off to my bedroom and screamed and cried into the pillow and by the time I had decided to re-appear downstairs, Darren had gone to work.

CHAPTER FIVE

Rose felt exhausted by the evening, thinking through the choices of what would be best for her children and the dilemma of how she was going to achieve it. But, the more she thought about it, the more reasons she found that prevented her from escaping.

Darren was at work and this gave Rose some time alone as the kids were tucked up in bed. She decided to text Tim, *'Hi, how are you? I've been playing kitchen with the kids and having a break for the day. Thank you for last night.'* Rose made herself a hot steaming mug of tea. Hugging the mug, she awaited Tim's reply.

Tim didn't take long to get back to her, he always had his phone close to him for his business. *'You don't have to thank me, glad you had a break. You must be exhausted. If you're free, can I call you after 7.30pm?'*

Rose blushed and had a huge smile on her face; it felt good that someone cared for her and knew what was going on. There was no way she could confide in her family anymore as Darren knew if she had talked to them. They would give him the cold shoulder even if they didn't mean to.

Rose was beginning to feel there was some kind of light at the end of the tunnel even if it was so far in the distance she couldn't quite see it clearly yet. It was all thanks to Tim treating her like a human; something so simple to change Rose's mood.

Rose decided to do some business emailing whilst waiting for her call from Tim. Rose loved her little business which she had set up through her own hobbies and ideas. She was naturally good at art just like her parents and she was super creative. Rose's business provided a gift service that was unique; from a box of chocolates to some flowers. It was called 'The Perfect Gift Co'. Her work was all handmade and Rose found it therapeutic and gave her mind a focus. The business was also a great 'here and now' escape from Darren; Rose would work in the dining room whilst Darren was in the living room watching the TV on an evening. 'Why didn't I think of this sooner'? Rose often thought, as the peace and quiet, talking to customers and friends had changed so much.

Rose set up the home business because of the strain Darren was putting on her working at a 'normal' job. After every shift there would be some sort of problem and he would interrogate her; it could be as simple as she had reapplied makeup or had given someone a lift home from work. The business was an escape for Rose; she had even managed to make some new friends with businesses which included some who were also mums. These new connections started to build her confidence in herself. Rose started to feel wanted and valued by others and was feeling emotional in different situations.

Rose had become used to not responding and would let comments from Darren go over her head and generally have a static feeling. She was becoming less like a robot and feeling more human-like. Rose found it was an easier life to live like a robot, but her identity was slipping and she had become more than just isolated.

Rose had lost some weight over the last couple of months and her fellow mums in business had started to compliment her. This was a rare feeling of success for Rose. It had also given her the confidence to realise that she didn't deserve what had been happening to her and she was re-gaining her self-worth.

Rose's iPhone rang and Tim's name flashed up. Rose jumped to her phone but let it ring a couple of times and then answered, "Oh, hi sorry, I was just emailing a few customers." Rose thought that would impress him.

"Hi, sorry I couldn't speak earlier, I was just finishing up in a meeting. I guess we're both busy with our businesses, eh?" Tim laughed along with Rose. Rose hadn't any idea on how to lead a conversation with someone she was falling for, it had been so long since she had to flirt.

"I've been thinking about last night," Rose spoke nervously and chewed her lip.

Tim, gentleman-like as he was, replied, "I meant what I said, I'm here for you no matter what." They spoke and giggled for a few minutes, Rose was in her bubble and wasn't thinking about anything else when Darren barged in and took the phone off her.

"Who's this?" Tim had clearly hung up. Darren had popped out of nowhere; Rose hadn't heard him sneak into the house.

Darren looked at Rose and demanded, "Who was it?" His glare pierced her skin for a moment before he grabbed her wrist and repeated himself and shouted so loud in her face. Rose closed her eyes and wished he wouldn't spray her with his spit. Rose felt that she should try and stand up for herself for once and not to be afraid. 'What's the worst he could do', she thought to herself.

"He's just a friend who's been helping me actually, and, we separated a few months ago so it doesn't matter who I talk to."

Darren threw her wrist back at her. "You disgust me! You haven't even left this house. What do I tell the kids when they wake up to a different man in the house every morning?" Rose didn't even answer, she felt that there was no point and it would be the same deluded answer yet again.

Rose had never slept with anyone whilst with Darren and yet he constantly accused her of doing so. Darren was overly paranoid and jealous and once had said that Millie-Rose could have been another man's child. Darren made her sound like a slut, someone who had a hundred men in the last week.

Rose lacked self-confidence and hated herself naked; in fact, she used to sleep with Darren with her pyjama top on because he made her small breasts seem non-existent and her little baby belly seem like she was the largest woman in the world. Darren's visions of Rose became hers and it didn't take long; Rose could barely look in the mirror and believed every word Darren said about her that was negative.

Darren had gone off in a huff shouting random comments and all Rose was thinking and worrying about was the children waking up and hearing everything that was going on.

There was a ring and it was coming from Rose's computer desk and she saw it was her business iPhone ringing. She looked down to see her personal one was smashed. Tim was calling her; she quickly ran over and answered it so it wouldn't ring anymore and hoped Darren hadn't heard it. 'Thank God there was another phone nearby', Rose thought.

Tim spoke, "Are you ok? I'm on my way, so don't worry."

Rose quickly squeezed out a few words, "Stay on the phone." She placed it in her pocket and kept it connected to Tim. Rose felt a little safer knowing that someone was on the end of the phone listening in.

Darren came barging in with Rose's pink hold-all with some of her clothes stuffed in it. "You can leave now – anything you don't take now, you won't get back."

Rose was in shock but held back her tears; she was going to be strong. "NO, I am not going, this is my home too. You have family nearby and mine are miles away so maybe you should go and then we can sort out the rest when the children aren't around." Rose couldn't believe she stuck up for herself for once and was putting her foot down but as soon as she had this confident streak, no sooner was Darren knocking it out of her. Clearly it was a weak attempt. "You left me and you moved out for a few nights a couple of weeks ago, so why don't you just go back to your mum's?"

Darren had turned his back on Rose and he went to the front door and threw her bag out onto the front yard as if to say, 'I'm the boss'. Darren had left her before and he didn't seem to have a problem with it.

Rose wished she had had the locks changed when she had the chance those 2 weeks ago. The police and housing association were not helpful. Tim had suggested she contact them and inform them of what was going on; both had responded with, "I'm sorry but it's his home too and he has a right to stay there so if you get the locks changed, we would have to allow entry." Somehow that didn't seem fair even when she explained what he was doing to her and that she had two under-fives in the house. The police had said she could report him and they would hold him but after four hours he would be released and able to return home, back to Rose and the children. Rose had started to lose faith in the police and couldn't find any services that would help. She had never felt so alone and afraid for her own safety.

Rose hadn't done anything about this before because Darren had not only threatened her, humiliated her, bullied her, intimidated her, emotionally abused her, harassed her, manipulated her, but he had cleaned her dry with a debt of £6,000 hanging over her shoulders. How was she meant to get out of this on her own? Rose often thought of suicide as her only escape but even that wasn't possible because she couldn't bear the thought of what might happen to her children; they were keeping her alive. Darren was clearly a very clever man to make someone feel like this and although uneducated, he wasn't thick; he had manipulated Rose so well that she had seen three counsellors about her behaviour as he made her believe it was her in the wrong and causing all these 'problems' in their marriage.

Darren had systematically discussed with Rose's close friends the lack of sexual contact he was getting from her. When this came out, Rose knew exactly what he was doing and felt a constant pressure to have sex with him. By the end of the relationship it had become robotic, like her emotions. Rose would just lay there and let him do what he needed to do. It was the excuse for talking to other girls behind her back or why he was in an ill-tempered mood; what choice was she given? There were times where she would go to the bathroom after and sob; she felt dirty and used.

Rose went outside and realised her pink hold-all wasn't by itself on the front lawn; Darren's dad, three sisters and two brothers were there. Rose's heart started to thump out of her chest; what was this? Assistance? What were they going to do? Rose remembered why she feared Darren and all those reasons why she kept her mouth shut and had started to doubt her decision to separate from him. Clearly it was more difficult than she thought it was going to be.

Darren's family did make Rose feel intimidated and it was worse for her because she knew what they were capable of; his dad had just been released from prison for assault on a police officer, his brother the prior year was held in custody for possible attempted murder, his sisters were all known to the police for nuisance and had ASBOs.

Rose never thought that Darren would get his family involved. Rose, who came from a working family would call the police only in an emergency and respect the authority they have. Darren's family seemed like a nightmare and a waste of tax payers' money and they knew what Rose thought as Darren told them 'what Rose's family was like'.

Rose's heart was pumping so hard as she looked at them all but was unable to look into their eyes; the street light caught them glaring at her. Rose's thoughts were going around her head like crazy; were they going to beat her up? Drag her down the street?

Smash up her things?

She thought about her precious children back in the house asleep oblivious, thankfully, to what was going on. A sharp stab went through her body and hit her heart. What would happen to them? Would she even be allowed to see them? Rose was trying her hardest not to show the fear she felt inside her. The anger was overcoming her and she thought about all she had done for Darren's family. She had been nothing but polite and helpful. She had helped create CVs so a couple of his family could apply for jobs, babysitting and even considered fostering when his sister's children were going to be taken away. Rose realised none of what she had done for them would mean anything; they were unappreciative and blood was thicker than water.

Within no time, Tim's flash car came speeding around the corner and made a sudden stop outside the house. Tim got out and asked, "Is everything ok, Rose?" Rose couldn't say a word. She was in a fog caused by her thoughts and fears, but then started to walk over to Tim.

Darren shouted over, "The boyfriend has come to help, has he? Like I said, get what you want now 'cause whatever you leave is left," and he laughed.

Rose could see all her fears of the reasons she had to stay come true and it wasn't a bad dream; this was happening right now but at least Tim was there with her, she kept telling herself. Darren's family stood in a line in front of the house like an army's frontline defence. Tim couldn't believe what he was hearing or seeing and even though Rose had told him most of the situation, it's hard to believe until you see it. Tim couldn't believe a human could treat another human like this and that Rose had even got into this situation; he believed she deserved much better. Tim put his hand on Rose's shoulder and said to her privately, "I'll help, don't worry, you can stay with me."

Rose had been given no option as they were outnumbered. Rose couldn't stand the thought of her children seeing anymore incidents involving Darren's verbal abuse. It was scaring them and clearly, if he wasn't going to leave, then she had no option; she was desperately trying to find the positives for her children.

Rose walked up to the house and walked in trying to keep her head held high. Tim was behind and was about to step foot into the house and assist Rose but Darren put out his arm and said,

"Sorry mate, I don't allow strangers into MY home."

Tim was concerned for Rose but she looked back at him with deep sad eyes and nodded, "Can you help put the things in the car from the front yard?" She spoke as calmly as she could. Tim nodded back and assumed his position by the front gate. Even Tim knew it was best not to speak up.

Twenty minutes of rushing upstairs and getting her things together, Rose was put under pressure from Darren's immature, chav-like sister, Katie, with her bright pink neon hair in a bun on the top of her head. The mouthy 16-year-old kept getting in Rose's way and saying things to Rose in a sarcastic tone.

"What are the kids meant to think? Mummy walked out on them? Is that who you've been shagging out there? I can see where that's going to go," and laughing in her face said, "you're scum. The kids are better off without you."

You would think Rose could ignore these childish comments but to her they cut deep; she wasn't leaving her children, she was being forced out. Rose knew what Katie was saying wasn't true and resisted the urge to say anything back in retaliation. She held back the tears building up and stinging her eyes, and answered back in her head, 'what do you know – you live in a gutter. My children don't need an auntie like you: a thief, a druggy, scum'.

Darren was lording about and watching his sister say all these things, with a huge Grinch smirk on his face. In a way, it made Rose realise that she had known what he was like all through the years. It wasn't just nothing or in her imagination.

Tim was hurt to see Rose in this mess; no one should have to go through this. Tim loaded the last of Rose's things and was thinking it was pain-free on the frontline. It had just started to spit rain on this mild evening and Rose walked out of the house one last time and started to get in the car before Darren spoke and said, "I'll need the key too." Rose wasn't going to give this up as this was still her house too.

Rose tried to get this across and said, "When the paperwork is through, I'll hand over the key." Who knew what would happen? She could get the house for all anyone knew (not that she particularly wanted to live there with all the negative memories).

Darren spoke again, coolly, "I need those keys now. How do I know you're not going to come in when I'm out?" and before Rose and Tim knew it, one of Darren's brothers, John, was coming towards them. Rose got in the car but he grabbed the door open. Tim had started the engine and began to rev so he could drive off quickly. Rose and Tim were running on adrenalin and were both scared. Thank goodness Tim was here with Rose.

What happened next was completely bewildering.

CHAPTER SIX

Tim had started to drive off but with the adrenalin and the shock and John pretty much hanging out the door, the car was jumping forward at a slow speed. Tim couldn't be responsible for his injury.

Tim had thought perhaps this insane brother would let go knowing it was dangerous enough but he didn't expect what happened next. John pulled on Rose so hard that she was ripped out of the car like a plaster off bare skin. Thank goodness Tim had only been going slow and did an emergency stop in the middle of the road. Rose stumbled up from the kerb side and had scrapes and marks all over her. John had succeeded in grabbing the keys out of her tight fist.

Tim got out of the car and rushed over to Rose who was about to head after John when Tim shouted, "They're not worth it," loudly so that it would be heard by Darren's family. Rose felt that those keys kept her safe and that she could get to her children if she needed to. It was her last hope. She had to know she could get to her children if she needed to and this made her even more fearful for them. Rose was in the road, crying against Tim when she felt a sick feeling overcome her and she took a deep breath and began to run towards Darren despite her terrified feelings.

"Give them back, give them back," she screamed, trying to prize them out of his hand. "It isn't just YOUR house!" Rose didn't know what she was doing, all she knew was she was fighting for some little hope. But, she looked pathetic and the years of keeping it cool had taken its toll on her. Tim was right, they weren't worth it but he didn't have the bond she had with her children. She believed she was in a war for right at this moment.

Rose was a slender lady and Darren was tall and shadowed Rose with his weight. She had no chance at getting anything from him. Tim had come over, and Darren said to him, "Tell her there's no point."

Tim didn't want to have to say this to Rose, but he did. "I agree, there is no point and it's only a key. Come on, I'll look after you." Rose looked at Darren's smirking face with disgust. She had never looked at him like this before. She had always been polite and smiled through gritted teeth.

Tim guided her back to the car but that wasn't all they had to endure. Jessica and another teenaged sister of Darren's had come up and started to spit on Rose and Tim like they were the scum of the earth. Rose had never been treated like this, like she was a rat in a sewer, and goose pimples came over her body.

Darren was laughing with his arms crossed, watching his sisters heckle them as they walked away. Rose got into Tim's car and he drove her out of the street, seeing in his mirror Darren's family cheering and jumping like it was the victory of a lynch mob. Neither Tim nor Rose had ever seen anything so weirdly crazy before.

As soon as they were out of sight, Rose bawled her eyes out, unable to control her tears. She wailed like someone had died and a part of her did with tears of both relief and pain for her children. Rose was shaking and uncontrollably crying so much that she had started to retch. Tim pulled over into a lay-by and Rose vomited in the grass verge; she didn't feel better from it, in fact she felt worse. She had a thumping headache making her roll her eyes back and unable to concentrate.

Tim had managed to calm Rose down after an hour of sitting in the car with Rose's most important possessions. It was all she had against her name, except her children. They discussed whether they should go to the police and report what had happened but decided against it at this time because Rose was in fear of what Darren might do in regards to the children. Tim's offer was still there and he welcomed Rose into his home like he said he would.

As soon as Rose went through the door, she ran to the downstairs toilet and was sick three times over. Tim was a gentleman and looked after her like she was a lost girl. He helped her to bed and sat with her whilst she cried herself to sleep; no words were shared, just the comfort of Tim stroking her hair.

Tim had been on his MacBook Pro for a little while working, when he took some time to Google 'help for women in domestic abusive relationships'. Tim knew what Darren was doing was not normal but had no idea how to talk to Rose about it, to be able to proceed and get some help. Tim thought that there surely was help available for Rose and her children and he came across the Women's Aid website with a quick tick box survey. He thought that if he got Rose to look over this and physically tick the boxes, then she would realise that it was not normal to be in this situation.

Rose was asleep for a few hours and turned over; the glow of Tim's MacBook had aroused her from her shallow sleep. Rose rubbed her eyes and through her tightly shut eyes she said, "What time is it?"

Tim replied, "Don't worry, it's only just gone midnight," and reached over to give her a kiss on the cheek.

Rose smiled and tried to peak through her eyes but the screen seemed like she was looking directly at the sun. She snuggled into Tim and asked him, "What are you working on at this time of night?" Tim thought it was better just to be honest and tell Rose what he was doing but he'd paused for too long. "Well??" Rose asked, smiling.

Tim put on his business head and got straight to the point, "I've found this website; why don't you take a look and do this check list?" Rose looked at him slightly curious and adjusted her eyes to try and see.

She read the header at the top of the webpage: 'Recognising domestic violence'. She looked at Tim and said, "Look, I am not a victim and I can look after myself."

Tim interrupted, "Why don't you sit up and just go through the check list and take each question one by one and I'll tell you why once you have completed it. Trust me, please."

Rose didn't want to do as Tim had requested but he had been so kind and she felt obliged so she sat up and popped her hair back into a pony tail to remove the thick wisps of hair blocking her sight. Rose felt a little nervous and didn't know why but she took a deep breath that she disguised as a sigh and took the MacBook from Tim.

Rose started to go through the check list:

> *1. Has your partner tried to keep you from seeing your friends or family?*
> Rose could tick a yes for that one, but that's ok it's not all going to be a yes and some people just want you all for themselves don't they?
>
> *2. Has your partner prevented you from continuing or starting a college course, or from going to work?*
> Oh! Rose could see a pattern already and she had only got to the second question. Well, she had to give up work but set up a business from home so he wouldn't have anything more to say.

Rose began to mumble along whilst filling in the yes/no survey. Tim was watching her as he knew that Rose needed to realise she was a victim.

> *3. Does your partner constantly check up on you or follow you?*
> Yes
>
> *4. Does your partner unjustly accuse you of flirting or of having affairs with others?*
> Yes
>
> *5. Does your partner constantly belittle or humiliate you, or regularly criticise or insult you in front of other people?*
> Yes
>
> *6. Are you ever afraid of your partner?*
> Yes… well these things are always vague and I mean there's reasons behind it; I think he is just very insecure.

She didn't want Tim to be right and was reassuring him that it wasn't that 'type' of relationship. Tim just listened and didn't say a word; he was ready and waiting for her patiently.

7. Have you ever changed your behaviour because you are afraid of what your partner might do or say to you?
>Yes

8. Has your partner ever destroyed any of your possessions deliberately?
>Yes

9. Has your partner ever hurt or threatened you or your children?
>Yes

10. Has your partner ever kept you short of money so you are unable to buy food and other necessary items for yourself and your children?
>Well, I guess I'm in debt for a reason, right?

Rose nervously laughed but then carried on with the questions with a look of despair on her face. Rose had now not bothered to look over at Tim because she was beginning to see that he was right even though she didn't want him to be.

11. Has your partner ever forced you to do something that you really did not want to do?
>Rose flushed red with this one and didn't want Tim to know why she had ticked yes.

12. Has your partner ever tried to prevent you from taking necessary medication, or seeking medical help when you felt you needed it?
>He didn't stop me from getting medication, but he also had me believe that I might be bi-polar and told me to seek counselling. I started to doubt myself and did follow his instructions; does that count?

13. Has your partner ever tried to control you by telling you that you could be deported because of your immigration status?

Rose felt a bit of relief as she could put a no next to this one, but Tim knew that she hadn't accepted the yes's she had put down so far and was still waiting for it to sink in.

14. Has your partner ever threatened to take your children away, or said he would refuse to let you take them with you, or even to see them, if you left him?

Tears began to fill Rose's big green eyes; had the penny nearly hit the ground?

Rose had started to hold her breath so that it held the gasps of air from the pain she could feel deep in the pit of her tummy. She could not shed that first tear as she would collapse into a devastating ball of tears.

15. Has your partner ever forced you to have sex with him or with other people? Has he made you participate in sexual activities that you were uncomfortable with?

Rose couldn't control it anymore, she used to be so good at being a robot and being numb. The tears were rolling down her face now and Rose kept trying to hold her breath to try and prevent Tim from seeing her in this state but there was no way she could. Tim already knew and he didn't care, as he knew this was coming, and was glad she was finally able to see the truth.

16. Has your partner ever tried to prevent your leaving the house?

Rose suddenly bawled her eyes out. It was a relief and finally Tim put his arm around her and pulled her into his embrace.

Tim stroked Rose's red silky hair which he knew calmed Rose and it took a good half an hour for her to stop bawling and start panting for breath.

When Rose looked at the bottom of the questionnaire and it read: *'If you answered yes to one or more of the above questions, this indicates that you may be experiencing domestic violence'*.

This started Rose off again. Rose hadn't just answered one question with yes but in fact all but one of the questions! It seemed too much for Rose to take. Tim didn't think she would answer that many yes's and was personally shocked, but he knew just by what Rose had shared with him that she could answer yes to a handful.

Tim was trying to stay strong for Rose but he hadn't realised just how much damage this man had done and was continuing to do to her. He was sensitive but 'cool' and couldn't stand to see anyone in a horrible situation.

Tim held her close and even tried to fight back his own tears. He saw Rose as a perfect mum trying to make a success out of herself even when she was faced with this. Tim didn't think Rose deserved this at all and he didn't know how to help or reassure her that everything was going to be ok but he had a brainwave. "I think it's going to be ok, there must be help here locally for victims."

Rose heard the word victim again and gave another wail of a cry. Tim continued, "No, I'm serious, there's got to be someone who could help or at least some system; we need to talk to a solicitor."

Rose's tears of hurt were turning into tears of happiness. It was a most peculiar mixture of emotions but she couldn't believe that Tim was looking after her and still willing to help when Rose thought that he wouldn't want to bring himself down to her level. Rose felt like she couldn't fight anymore; she had done it for 6 years already and that was far more than enough.

Tim kept trying to reassure her, "It's going to be ok; we can draw up a plan on how to sort this out. I'm with you all of the way. You need some rest now, though."

"I can't get any sleep now, all I can think about is everything he has done to me and if he's capable of that, then how on earth am I going to get my kids back?" Rose was starting to pant in panic. She realised that if Darren was so clever to have her believe that their life was 'normal', then he would be capable of anything.

"Shhhh," Tim put his finger against her lips, "you need to calm down, I'm going to make you a cup of tea and we will put something on the TV; we can get your mind off it somehow."

Tim left Rose in the bed hugging the covers and he proceeded with his plan of making her a cup of tea. When Tim returned, he put the TV on and switched it to the comedy channel which had 'Friends' on it, a light-hearted background programme to ease the tension. Rose smiled at him in thanks.

It had taken a couple of hours for Rose to calm down and enjoy just watching the TV. She was so tired her mind had become empty and she eventually fell back to sleep. Tim stayed awake to keep an eye on her, he didn't want her waking up upset and being too polite to wake him; it was more important that he looked after her now more than ever.

Reference- [1]

---

[1]https://www.womensaid.org.uk/the-survivors-handbook/am-i-in-an-abusive-relationship

CHAPTER SEVEN

Rose woke up at lunch time the next morning with a pounding headache and dry mouth; she had never slept this long since before Millie-Rose was born. Next to her on the bedside table she saw a glass of fresh orange, a glass of water, a cup of tea and a cup of coffee that Tim had made for her. Rose could hear some pottering about going on downstairs and she put on Tim's robe that was hung up behind the door and went to investigate. Tim was cleaning up and had breakfast ready to cook.

"I didn't know what you would like so I got everything. Cooked breakfast? Croissants? Cereal?"

Rose blushed and smiled as she looked and saw the selection; she felt so cared for instantly. It was an unusual feeling for her and overwhelming at the same time but Rose had started to become familiar with this caring treatment.

Tim spoke again, "Is that my robe?" Rose smiled again and went over to Tim and gave him a kiss on the cheek. "What was that for?"

Rose replied, "For being my hero and pretty much rescuing me."

Tim frowned back and then whispered to her, "I haven't finished rescuing you yet."

Rose couldn't swoon any more than she was already; Tim was becoming more and more her knight in shining armour. She didn't believe in fairy-tales or on-screen romances, but she was beginning to see that it could be real. Rose was intrigued to know what Tim meant but didn't feel able to ask and thought it may have just been a figure of speech; she had learnt to never expect anything from anyone and that was rooted deep.

Rose bent over the kitchen counter and grabbed a crumpet; food was a good distraction after what happened last night. Rose sat down at the breakfast bar and Tim waited on her hand and foot and treated her like a princess. Rose couldn't stop smiling, even if she had deep sad eyes.

Tim thought Rose had woken up completely different to how last night had ended; he loved to see her smile and wondered what had put the spring in her step this morning as he hadn't seen her like this, ever. Tim went over and sat beside Rose. She was taking her time eating her crumpet at the breakfast bar and Tim stroked her back slowly, "Are you ok?" he asked with a smile.

Rose looked at Tim, smiled and replied, "There's a way out, I know there is! What you said last night, well, we can research it can't we?" Tim was relieved to see a much more confident Rose.

"Of course! Now let's finish our breakfast," and he gave her a kiss on the cheek.

Rose got dressed eventually; she seemed to be in a bubble of thoughts and eventually asked Tim, "Could you possibly take me to my dad's? I guess I'm going to have to talk to my family and my dad knows some of what's been going on."

Tim responded, "You don't have to ask." Rose hugged him in thanks and they planned to go the next day. Tim had rearranged some meetings and had his staff get on with running the business for the next few days.

Rose and Tim spent a couple of hours sorting out Rose's things so they weren't all over the place and Rose was feeling a little more relaxed; a neat freak needs to know where things are. Later that evening, Tim took Rose out for a meal to take her mind off things and a to be in a different atmosphere.

Rose was soon welcoming her bed when she got back and ended up throwing up all of her meal before she got there. Tim was starting to worry about her as she was having splitting headaches and he could see the stress taking its toll on her. Rose had bloodshot eyes and even though she made an effort for Tim he could see her sad eyes were going over and over the events of the previous night. Rose had changed from the confident thinking woman this morning to the self-doubting Rose she was; he had noticed she got worse as she got tired and her confidence slipped into nothingness.

Tim had soon decided he needed to nurse her and brought her his remedy that solved his headaches and feeling rough and that was soluble codeine. It probably wasn't best to depend on it like he did when he was stressed out but he couldn't afford to feel rough. Rose drank it, no questions asked, as paracetamol didn't touch the edge and she could barely swallow it or would throw it up soon after taking it. Rose managed to settle after an hour and Tim kept an eye on her whilst she drifted off to sleep.

The next day they set off in the morning to Liverpool; it would take just two hours to get there. It was a cool day with a chilly breeze but this was welcoming to Rose. Rose was feeling anxious but secretly Tim was too; it was Tim's birthday and he had changed his plans to help Rose. He didn't really celebrate it and somehow he was now wrapped up in her world.

Rose slept most of the journey and they stopped so that Rose could throw up again half way there; Tim was making sure she was having a lot of water to replace what she was losing. He was truly a gentleman and looking after her.

When they arrived at Liverpool, they decided to stop for some lunch at a café Rose used to always go to. The staff had clearly changed over but it was overwhelming being there as it had been over two years since she had even set her feet back in Liverpool. She had missed out on her grandfather's funeral and a dear family friend's funeral along with a cousin's wedding too. Rose realised just how isolated she had become and it was going to take some getting used to being back in contact with family and friends and not having to worry about every word that she would speak and every excuse that she needed to give. The reality kept on hitting Rose and she tried to keep sucking in the tears especially because if she cried her head felt like it would implode.

Tim and Rose enjoyed a light lunch until two familiar faces walked through the café door: Rose's two aunts. Auntie Lucy and Auntie Laura were very close and were always close to Rose, or at least until she left for University in York and met Darren. The two aunts were in shock to see Rose and also with a gentleman they had never met. They both screamed with excitement and went over and hugged the life out of Rose; they both couldn't get over seeing her like this.

Lucy and Laura could only be described as the chuckle sisters, they were always giggling together and cheered anyone up that spoke to them; the perfect people to bump into at this moment in time for Rose. They of course didn't ask, and pulled up a pew and joined Rose and Tim. Lucy went over to order a couple of lattes for her and Laura and rushed back over so she didn't miss any of the conversation that was taking place at the table. Rose was so excited to see them and it felt like she was back at home but she didn't know how on earth she was going to get through the conversation without gasps and drama splashed into the situation.

Lucy sat back down and smiled over at Rose and said, "So, are you going to introduce us to your…" and coughed mid-sentence, "…friend?" Rose knew full well that the emphasis on 'friend' was a false motive question.

Rose smiled back and responded, "Sorry, of course; this is Tim and he is a business connection I made through my company and has basically befriended me and offered his support."

Tim held out his hand to offer a handshake to Lucy and Laura, which they were very impressed with and looked knowingly at Rose: 'what a gentleman' and raised their eyebrows.

Rose thought, why not just cut to the chase because they will find out one way or another anyway, and so she took a deep breath and began to tell them exactly what Tim was helping with and what had happened, finally closing up with, "…so I guess Tim is keeping me from being homeless right now."

Rose managed to tell them in brief and without her aunts disturbing her for more information which is what they usually did. Lucy and Laura were gripped on every word and couldn't believe this had happened to their niece. Not only this but Laura worked with the council and knew some of the in's and out's about social services. Lucy was reapplying her bright red lipstick after guzzling her latte through Rose's update. Laura was thinking council-minded and was dressed like it today too (she must be going to work, Rose thought).

Laura asked with a hint of demand, "So, what's your plan to get the kids back then? They can't live with him. They need to be with their mother!"

Rose replied, "Well, we have spoken about it briefly but I guess we are going to look for a solicitor and fight it in court. I suppose it's why we are here today too."

Laura's eyes widened and shook her head, "No, no, no!"

Rose was thinking – 'oh no, here we go' – she had already found it hard to tell the short version of what had happened and tried so hard to not think of her feelings within this but had a very big lump in her throat.

Laura was concerned. "Look, if those children are without you for long then they will stay at their dad's house and what if the courts take months or years? You won't have a leg to stand on! You need to get those kids back now before time passes and it's too late."

Rose wasn't expecting this and it actually started to make her panic but she remained calm and said, "But, how am I meant to do this? I have no money. Darren has basically got me into £6,000 worth of debt which is on my shoulders at the moment. He was always refused credit and begrudged paying anything for the petrol or for the kids. I have no money to my name whatsoever and I will not get a house or anything."

Rose was welling up and thought that no one understood just what a mess this was for her, her credit report was sure to be badly damaged. Darren was clever and had gotten her into this situation so that she couldn't escape. She had used her auntie's inheritance to buy furniture for the house and this was all gone now. Rose couldn't stand living on second hand furniture for any longer and so had used her own money to have a nice home because Darren clearly wasn't going to. Later, into the end of the relationship, he had started using his wages to go out clubbing three times a week and on video games. Rose had constantly found it a struggle in the relationship to keep her head above water as Darren would only help if it was a last resort; he was completely in control.

Laura and Lucy spoke at the same time, "We'll help you." Tim was shocked at what he was hearing; this day was turning around already, and he could see Rose was going through an emotional turmoil and didn't want to get her hopes up.

Tim spoke too. "And, you know I'm here for you and I will help in whatever way I can."

Rose spoke and said, "Would we be able to live at yours for a bit, Tim? I know it's a lot to ask and I probably shouldn't have blurted it out in front of my aunts."

Tim didn't want to do this now but he had to. "The house isn't mine, Rose." Rose was taken aback.

63

"Oh?"

"It's not mine, it's my parents' place and they are away at the moment. They get back from holiday in a week. I didn't tell you because I didn't want you to panic about staying over and I can talk to my parents about you, but I'm not sure about the kids."

Laura and Lucy looked at each other, and Lucy spoke, "Look, Tim's clearly trying to help you and you've been through enough without us knowing the finer details."

Tim smiled in thanks. "And I will look after you Rose, in fact if you need a place to stay I will help you find a place, help you move and if you want me to stay with you for a bit then I will do that; I am here for you."

Rose had spoken about being afraid of being on her own in a house in case Darren were to find her. Lucy and Laura were talking amongst themselves by now and Tim was holding Rose's hand and reassuring her. He could see her thoughts were rushing around in her head over and over; Tim could read her like an open book.

They all had a sip of their hot drinks and then Laura spoke, "I am happy to give you £500 to help towards a deposit on a house and I have some furniture that you're welcome to have."

Rose choked on her drink and then her second auntie spoke, "I am also happy to match it with another £500 and that should complete a deposit and I have some cutlery you're welcome to."

Rose burst out in tears, "I can't take money off you like that! I haven't seen you in two years! Why would you do that?" Everyone in the café was looking in their direction and Tim put his arm around Rose and passed her a serviette to dry her tears.

Laura spoke again, "Look, we know why you haven't seen us and nothing changes that you are family; those kids need to be with you." Both aunts got their cheque books out and wrote Rose a cheque for £500 each. Rose was in shock; one-minute smiling, and the next sobbing into Tim's arms.

Lucy was welling up and trying not to cry for her niece; she couldn't believe Rose was in this situation in the first place.

After they had talked about Tim and what he did along with general chit chat, Rose and Tim left to head to Rose's father's apartment. Rose was anxious at what he might think of all of this and hated to be the bearer of bad news. She was always conscious of her parents thinking that she was a failure.

Tim hadn't seen Rose smile for a while and as she was chatting in the car on the way to her dad's, she had this glow and for the first time a confidence boost. "Oh my gosh Tim, can you believe it! I really wasn't expecting that," and giggling, "I can really get out of this now and with Millie-Rose and Harrison! What do you think my dad will say? Or my mum – hmmm, but I don't care because for once I feel like I'm getting somewhere. Did this really happen?" Rose kept reliving everything in her head and it was nice enough seeing her aunts, never mind the offer of money to help.

They soon arrived at her father's apartment. He was in the top flat and he always called it the penthouse even if it was just the third floor. Rose's dad was in his late fifties and always liked to keep up to date with technology which was not always a good thing because when things did go wrong it was hard to explain how to fix the problem.

Rose's dad, Alfie, had whispery grey and black hair, lovely dark brown square rimmed glasses, a long face just like Rose had and always dressed in jeans and a shirt; he took pride in his appearance. As soon as he answered the door, Rose flung her arms around him and they both were in tears. They hadn't seen each other for more than two years and that was an issue because Rose was daddy's little girl. Despite what age she would get, they would always be very close. When Rose remembered, she introduced Tim to him, yet Alfie was rightly sceptical. Tim shook his hand in his gentlemanly manner. They both were welcomed into the 'penthouse' and sat down on the chocolate brown leather sofa as Alfie made them a specialised coffee with his new technology coffee machine. He could do an advert for this coffee company, he was that good at it and demonstrated just how easy and quick it made a rich smooth latte.

Alfie then cut to the chase. "So, go on then, you only come over if there's something that has happened?" And he let Rose explain the whole story without interrupting. She had never been listened to this much in a long time. He did know of some of the elements as Rose used to go out and walk Darren's sister's dog for her and she was able to quickly phone her dad. So even though it had been two years in distance, they were still very much in the loop and as close as ever.

Once Rose had explained everything, including the plan that was coming together rather quickly, he spoke and said, "I did tell you to have a long engagement. I always thought Darren was weird and even though I don't talk to your mother, I know she did too…but I guess you didn't have much of an option and it looks like Tim is bringing my daughter back home," and smiled at him in thanks. "I am happy to match your aunties and give you £500 too."

Rose sighed, "Oh, Dad…" and cried on his shoulder. Alfie was always straight to the point with no messing about. "Tim, I expect you to look after her and I know I don't have to ask because you've already done such a good job."

Rose again was talking and talking about it and just wondered how on earth this had happened, she couldn't believe it! "This is life-changing," she said and then snoozed in the car as Tim drove her back to her temporary home.

What everyone hadn't thought about is just how she was going to get the children and to have them live with her. Darren wasn't going to just hand them over so they could live with her. Rose knew that the children were the biggest key to the control he still had over Rose. He loved the feeling of power.

CHAPTER EIGHT

The following weeks consisted of Rose and Tim acting as if they were in episodes of CSI. There was paperwork spread all over the dining table. From solicitor's info to police record numbers to the new house information they had found and put a security deposit on. They had found a house in Liverpool right in the centre of where Rose's family lived. The decision to move here was: 1. For the family support and 2. For Rose and the children's safety. Tim had even agreed to make this move with Rose and move in with her and the children. Rose couldn't believe it and was running on adrenalin.

The police had become heavily involved and had even put dates together of when Rose should flee with the children and the police placed it on their alert system. To get the answers Rose needed was very difficult; solicitors cost £100 to answer just one question and she had no money with it all being invested into the deposit of the house. Charities didn't have a definite answer as they could only advise them and this was the same with the Citizens' Advice Bureau.

The question they wanted an answer to was, 'would one or both of us get arrested or investigated for kidnap'? Rose had given up on searching on Google; it's true the children had been with their father in the former marital home for only a few weeks by the time they were planning to flee, but Rose was their mother. Eventually the police were the route for answers and they reassured Rose and Tim that this was not the case as parental responsibility was on both parents and there was no custody or court order in place to prevent it.

Tim was concerned for himself and a potential kidnapping charge. He wanted everything to go to plan and smoothly. It was also a lot of money if it went wrong. Rose's family had all been in contact with her and they had a list of where furniture was coming from. They had planned a time slot on when they could pick it up in the removal van they hired. It was the coming weekend when they had planned to flee and Rose was very anxious that it all went to plan. Tim was reassuring her but he also was feeling the anxiety of the situation; what if Darren found out their plan?

Tim and Rose had a rough schedule in place: first to move everything they had across to the new house and pick up the keys, then go with the van to their parents' and Rose's family members houses for all this furniture they had been offered. Secondly they would stay over for the night so they could set up the house and be back at Tim's parents' house for the following evening where they would stay. Thirdly, the final part of the plan would be to pick up the kids on Rose's 'access day' on the Saturday and to head straight over to the house and seek refuge.

Rose felt it was best to do it all within two days because she couldn't risk Darren finding out and refusing her to see the children at all. Thank goodness she was given 'access days' even though the only reason Rose had these were due to Darren needing a break from the children. Rose had technically looked after them solely since Millie-Rose was born so it was completely alien for him to be taking the reins, even if it meant having a power trip over Rose.

Rose was at Tim's parents' house on the night before the big move. Rose had gotten to know them in such a short space of time and they thought she was a delightful young woman with prospects and gumption. They had tea together. Tim's mum, Sarah, had cooked a banquette but Rose was certainly not hungry as she was so anxious; she was shaking and throwing up every ten minutes with a pounding headache. They had gone through the plan over and over again; they had discussed all outcomes and then suddenly Rose's phone vibrated and was showing a text from Darren.

'Hi Rose, I don't think Harrison is well enough to see you tomorrow as he has gotten worse this last week. Millie-Rose could come and Harrison could stay with me.'

Rose immediately started to panic and panted and was shaking even more now. Tim came by her side and helped her gain control of her breath whilst he passed her phone to his dad, James.

Thoughts took over Rose, "He knows our plan! Why would he not allow Harrison to see his mummy, it will make him feel better? You told me Tim, that this would happen and he would start to control me... that's it, the plan has gone down the pan." Tim was rubbing her back and his mum had gone to make her a cup of tea and get her a glass of water.

It didn't take long to listen to what Tim and his parents had to say on the matter because Rose was so out of breath from mumbling away and panicking that she needed to stop for a moment. It was simple for Rose to reply back and explain it would still be a good idea for Harrison to come as she is his mother and she could offer the comfort he needs and could act on any medical needs. It was only a couple of weeks ago she had taken him to the doctor on her 'access day' because she could see he had conjunctivitis and Darren hadn't taken him.

There were a few nerve wracking responses, but eventually Darren said he would see how he was in the morning. Rose was very anxious and didn't want anything to go wrong.

This meant that Rose had hardly any sleep that night but finally the day had come and Rose drove her old green Ford Fiesta to pick up the kids; her heart was racing and she had already been sick in the morning twice over. Rose was getting fed up of feeling this ill and not being able to keep any of her food down. She felt like she had lived with a hangover for the last few weeks but she knew it was because she cared and loved her children so much that she couldn't bear the thought of this plan not going right. It meant living every day like a nightmare.

Tim was waiting for her at his parents' house and was talking to her over hands-free to calm her down. All she had to do was get through the next few minutes without giving the game away.

Before Rose drove around the corner of the street, she got her phone ready in her pocket and on record; this was needed just in case anything was said or done. The situation was hard enough to understand. Rose took one last breath as she pulled up in front of her old home which was already looking run down. She confidently opened her car door and walked up the driveway. Rose had her red hair down for the first time; she had made herself look 'normal' compared to the green/yellow skin colour she had adopted.

The front door opened as she approached and there stood Millie-Rose with her rucksack on and smiling. She saw Rose and nearly knocked her over as she ran to her and gave her the biggest squeeze of a hug. Rose hugged her back in joy and relief; she was in her arms and like a birthday present not to be taken off her. Rose belted Millie-Rose up in her pink car seat and then went to pick Harrison up. He was in Darren's arms and looked seriously ill. Rose couldn't believe it. Harrison's eyes were so gluey and nearly sealed shut. He was very red cheeked and hot and with a pale, washed-out face. When he saw his mummy, he tried to wriggle out of his dad's arms and climb over to Rose. As soon as Harrison attached himself to Rose, he wept and snuggled into her neck to smell her; Harrison always smelt his mummy for comfort.

Rose asked Darren, "So, have you taken him to the doctor's?" and his reply was, "No, you know how these things work, they clear up in time."

Rose held onto what she wanted to say and thought about the end goal which was in her arms and car right now. "What medicine has he taken this morning so I know when to give him some?"

Darren's response was, "None yet, I was going to mention to you he needs some." Rose had heard enough and put Harrison in the car with his comfort blanket and he managed to calm down. She told the kids to 'say goodbye to your dad'. Harrison didn't bother waving and Millie-Rose was more concerned with what they were going to be doing and telling Rose she had been playing doctor and trying to help Harrison.

Rose drove away and loved the feeling; she was going to make Harrison better and she was going to give them a happy life and love and care for them like she had been yearning to do for these last few long weeks.

Rose felt for Harrison and felt partially to blame but as Tim kept saying, "What else can you do? You have taken him to the doctor's yourself and Darren hasn't followed through with the medicines. You have done what was possible and the best with what you can." Rose didn't feel comforted at all by these words; she believed as their mum, that anything that happened to them was her fault.

Rose's heart was still racing and her hands were shaking as she phoned Tim on her iPhone on the loudspeaker to let him know that it had gone smoothly and she was coming to pick him up and 'zoom, zoom'.

Millie-Rose was talking away in the background and poor Harrison was cuddling his blanket at the same time as smiling at his mummy. Rose was watching him in the driver's mirror, he really didn't look well. "We are going to have to go straight to the hospital, Harrison is really not well," Rose informed Tim while trying to remain positive so Millie-Rose wouldn't get upset.

It didn't take long for Rose to get to Tim and pick him up. He took one look at Harrison and jumped into the car like there was a hot potato in his pants. "We're going to have to drive to Liverpool to the hospital because if he is admitted here, then who knows what will happen?" Tim advised as best as he could and Rose hadn't thought about what would happen if Harrison did have to be admitted.

Rose set off with no time to spare. Tim could see by his feet a plastic bag with some fruit shoots, sandwiches, bananas and apples in it and smiled because he knew Rose would of course have been organised and prepared for anything. The journey felt like it was never-ending to Rose and Tim. They could hear Harrison wheezing and Millie-Rose seemed to be getting concerned too as he wasn't talking back to her. Rose told Millie-Rose the plan and that they were going to stay with Mummy and Tim for now and would see if they could get a doctor to look at Harrison.

Millie-Rose was completely thrilled with the idea of living with Mummy and Tim. "I'm so excited, can I stay with you forever?"

Rose knew she couldn't answer this because who would know what was going to happen next. More than anything, she wanted to shout: 'YES' and reassure Millie-Rose.

Two hours had passed and they had just gone through the tunnel when they saw a police station and Rose pulled in. "We had better do this first to save our own backs, we don't know what is going to happen."

Rose left Tim and the children in the car and walked up to the entrance of the police station. She pressed the buzzer and waited for an answer. Time slowed down to what seemed to be a halt and Rose started to daydream about a happy ending, all the while fretting that she needed to get Harrison to see a doctor.

Five minutes later and someone spoke in a squeaky telephone voice, "Yesss, how can we help?"

Rose came out of her trance and didn't know where to start. "Erm,,,,well you see, I have my two children in the car, I have picked them up from their dad's and I don't plan on taking them back. It's kind of a long story, and, errr, oh yeah, the Yorkshire police have assisted me and I have some police numbers I can reference to."

There was a loud sigh and the lady's squeaky voice replied, "There will be someone with you shortly," and another long five minutes went by.

Rose looked over to the car; she could see Tim handing the kids a fruit shoot and it seemed there was no reason to worry. A middle-aged blonde police officer came to the doors and said, "I'm just a traffic officer but I'm going to make some checks on the log numbers you have, if that's ok?" and she ushered Rose into the entrance hall.

Rose nervously replied, "Thank you so much; the police in Yorkshire said to hand ourselves over, so to speak, so you're prepared at this end in case their dad rings up later. There is something else though, my son is very ill and I need to take him to hospital as soon as I can. I would have gone there first, but I knew I had to do this as we may be at the hospital for hours."

The police officer looked over her spectacles and she enquired, "Where are the children now?"

Rose replied, "They are just outside in the car with my friend waiting for me." She popped her head outside the entrance and could see the three of them waiting in the car parked closest.

"Ok, I will log this for now and you head to the hospital. If there's any more information we need we will get in touch; I'm assuming all your details are on the log numbers?" she asked.

Rose replied, "Yes they are," she shuffled in her bag, "and here are their birth certificates if you need them at all."

The officer smiled at Rose and took the certificates out of her hand. "I will just quickly photocopy these and log it so it's on file."

While Rose waited for her to come back, she sent a quick text to Tim asking, *'Is everything ok? Nearly done and then we can shoot off xx.'*

Tim replied almost instantly, *'Kids are fine, don't worry, just concentrate on this part and then we can get onto the next x.'*

Surprisingly the police officer was really quick and handed over the certificates to Rose and wished her well. It was nice to not feel judged and spoken to politely. Rose felt ashamed even to have to be in the police station and hand herself over.

Rose jogged back to the car with Tim and the kids waiting eagerly for her. Millie-Rose asked, "What was you doing, Mummy?"

And Rose replied, "Just an errand, nothing to worry about. Now let's get Harrison to the hospital shall we? You're doing a good job of looking after him, Millie."

Millie-Rose grinned with pride and Rose grinned back thinking what a credit her children were to her.

Rose looked over at Harrison and he was asleep but snorting each time he breathed in, a clear struggle even if he did sound like a cute little piggy.

Tim reassured her, "They have been fine and we have been singing different songs together and Millie-Rose has been teaching me new ones. But, come on let's get going. I'll drive, so let's swap places." They changed position and Tim could see the emotional affect it was having on Rose. She was becoming tired and drained.

It wasn't long before they arrived at the hospital and they parked in the car park and hurried into A&E. Rose was carrying Harrison asleep on her shoulder; she held him like he was the most precious thing in the whole world to her because her worry had gone past concern. They signed in at the reception and Rose explained in short what was wrong and why and also asked if anyone rang the hospital asking about Harrison to not let them know they were here.

Finally, they sat down and then came more waiting. Millie-Rose stuck by her mum like a leach and Rose could see the emotional strain that was taking place in her little girl and boy yet they had no idea how the guilt was making her feel sick.

Rose constantly felt guilty, ashamed, a bad mother, confused and upset from the past years of her life and that she had allowed her children to be subjected to him. All Rose could think about while sitting in A&E was everything that had happened and the memories kept flashing up in her mind like a whirlwind.

* * *

It had been a long night of teething for Harrison and I must have had about 3 hours' worth of sleep split up into smithereens so I found it a little difficult to get up when Millie-Rose called from her room. I gave Darren a polite nudge considering he hadn't been too much help in the night. He got out of bed like a whippet and I wasn't expecting that. There must be something wrong already. I rolled my eyes back and enjoyed spreading out in the bed until I heard him scream at Millie-Rose like she had done something unforgivable.

"HOW DARE YOU DISRESPECT OUR HOUSE LIKE THIS!"

What on earth had she done, I thought and why on earth was he speaking to her like this?

"NOW YOU CAN WASH THIS UP."

I just kept thinking that Millie-Rose was only 2 1/2 and she didn't understand; it was most likely my fault. I got out of bed because I knew I would have to intervene and he was more likely doing this for a reaction out of me than taking whatever it was seriously. I did a fast walk to Millie-Rose's room and I could hear Harrison screeching. Darren must have frightened him. I looked in her room and could see pen all up the walls and she was in tears and started to walk towards me.

"Have you seen this???" Darren asked me.

"Yes, I have but I think you're a little out of tone." I turned to Millie-Rose and went to pick her up for a hug; she sobbed on my shoulder and was confused and then my hand went hot and I realised she wet herself on me. I was so angry at Darren. How could he do this to her? She had no idea that this was wrong and it was my fault, I left the pens in her bedroom by accident.

Darren had slammed the door and walked off; he was annoyed I'd gone and comforted her. He had no idea. I gave Millie-Rose a bath whilst I had Harrison in my sling. This had become a life saver for episodes like this and for a lot of the time I was left to sort them both out. I didn't mind, I would rather sort them both out now because it was easier to avoid these situations and I felt guilty because I could have just gone to her room in the first place. I started to tell myself, 'sleep deprivation will not get to me…sleep deprivation will not get to me…sleep deprivation will not get to me'.

As soon as Millie-Rose was born, there was something held against me and she was used as a tool to keep me. It was like someone had locked me up and threw away the key. I was like a single mum in this family home and Darren seemed to be non-existent as a father. The more time went on, the more apparent this was the case. I didn't mind to be honest; it was nicer that he wasn't at home. I remembered I felt this over-protective love for my children and that it was my duty to protect them from him too, even if that meant taking a hit from him. Darren hardly ever hurt me but the threats and the times he had was enough for me to 'behave'. Sometimes I wished he would just hit me and get it over and done with because the tension was too much for me to take. I was stressed out and couldn't sleep.

* * *

Rose was daydreaming, as she did when emotions were high, and she didn't hear the nurse when she called out Harrison's name. Tim had to give her a nudge. Rose got up in a rush and ushered the kids into the cubicle to be seen.

The nurse was young and could see Harrison wasn't well and asked the question, "So what is wrong with Harrison today?"

Rose explained the story that they had been with their dad but they had fled. She had noticed the deterioration and explained she had taken Harrison to the doctor's on her 'access day', but clearly he hadn't gotten any better and suspected his dad had not treated the conjunctivitis as advised. Rose spoke in a fast, panicky voice and the nurse did a full examination of Harrison and asked if he had any allergies before giving him some paracetamol. She asked for them to sit in the waiting room again for the doctor.

Rose, Tim and both children had barely touched the seats when the doctor called Harrison's name, which was unusual as normally there would be a long wait. Rose immediately thought that the young nurse may have judged her on the spot and would think it was in fact her fault and not Darren's. She was embarrassed to be there and to have to justify herself to everyone they came across.

They headed straight into another cubicle and the doctor asked for Harrison to be stripped down to his nappy for his assessment. Rose followed the instructions and the doctor checked him over and Rose had to repeat her story once again, with her head held low with shame. The doctor said that Harrison would have to be admitted to the ward and would be staying overnight. He said the consultant would see him in the morning but confirmed he had clear conjunctivitis, a chest infection and an ear infection which had gotten out of control.

The doctor was kind with Rose and was reassuring to her but Rose just felt this huge guilt that she had let her baby boy get so ill. The doctor checked his oxygen levels and they were down in the 60's '...and the normal level should be at least 95', he cautiously informed Rose.

She burst into tears and Tim took over and asked all the necessary questions of the doctor. Rose was in a blurry fuzz and couldn't hear what was being said. She held Harrison close and didn't know what would have happened if they hadn't managed to get the children today and to the hospital. Her mind was spinning with horrible thoughts and thanked God that they had this plan in place. Rose was so thankful that she had her children now and that she could do the best for them.

That night Harrison was admitted to a ward; it seemed to take forever and they still had Millie-Rose with them who was getting tired and bored; she had done so well and behaved all this time. Harrison needed to be put onto oxygen but he refused to put on the mask. The nurse tried to change the filter so it was the oxygen that pops into his nose but Harrison had a screaming fit and made himself sick. When you're not feeling well you don't want a mask shoved onto you or something put up your nose. In the end, Tim said he would have Harrison on his knee and hold the mask until he fell asleep and then he would put him in the cot. Rose wanted to help and comfort him herself but she had Millie-Rose to think about and she needed to look after her. After all, the children had only met Tim on a handful of occasions so it was lucky Harrison even took to him.

Millie-Rose had fallen asleep on Rose and Tim had Harrison on his knees. They were both uncomfortable sat on the hard plastic chairs. Harrison wouldn't wear the oxygen mask, so Tim had to strategically hover it over near his mouth whilst he slept. Every time Tim thought he could get away with putting it on, Harrison screamed to high heavens and every time Tim nodded off, Harrison would slip and wake up. Both Tim and Rose had given up on the idea of sleep and even an option of a cat nap seemed to be out the window too; luckily they both had their iPhones to watch TV on and they shared a headphone.

The next morning Harrison was already improving and looked like he had a bit more life in him. Harrison happily went into the hospital cot and they both anticipated waiting for the consultant to come and update them on what was going on. They were worried as throughout the night, the nurses kept on coming to check on Harrison and not the other children in the ward.

CHAPTER NINE

Three days had passed and Rose and Tim had stayed in hospital with Millie-Rose to watch over Harrison. Auntie Lucy and Auntie Laura had helped look after Millie-Rose throughout the stay and that allowed Tim and Rose to have some sleep on the very uncomfortable plastic hospital chairs.

Rose wouldn't leave his side; she was in fear that Darren was going to pop out of nowhere and take him from his hospital cot. Harrison's oxygen levels were taking a long time to come back up to the normal levels and it was confirmed that he had untreated bronchitis and asthma alongside the untreated conjunctivitis and ear infection. Rose was shocked with just a few weeks of being apart from her children that this could happen.

The doctors had written the discharge note finally and noted it was due to neglect. Whilst in hospital, Rose received a couple of phone calls from the police and she had expected this. Thankfully Rose had booked an appointment with a local solicitor's whilst in hospital as she wanted to start the divorce as soon as possible. Rose wanted to be released completely from him and to feel free and not under his control. She didn't want to have his surname any longer. It had dawned on her just how her life was and how she felt trapped, imprisoned, isolated, intimidated and manipulated and much more. It was overwhelming and exhausting but Rose had no choice but to carry on; she had no idea how she was going to pay the solicitor but thankfully they offered a free thirty-minute consultation and at least this would give her an idea of where she stood and what the process might be.

That afternoon Rose went to the solicitor's office on her own; she was a little more relaxed at the thought of the children being in the new house and Harrison on the appropriate medication and with Tim watching over him. Rose filled out the form and happily ticked the box for 'divorce' and was thinking about her future and just how much it was already changing. She still wondered if there could be an easy resolution to this mess.

The wait seemed to take some time; Rose was beginning to get anxious and feeling a nervous itch to get what needed to be done – done! Rose checked her phone, whenever there was free time she did some quick networking on different social media platforms for her business. Rose felt for Tim and his business and knew that at the moment he would be taking this time off but would have to either commute to the office or relocate, but again there were staffing issues; Tim had told her not to think on it but Rose was a natural worrier and took it all on-board.

Rose noticed an email that just came through and it was from Darren; her heart immediately plummeted just like she was back under his control. There was nothing written, just an attachment. Rose didn't know what to think as she waited for her 3G to load up the PDF and was baffled by what she read from York County Court and Family Court.

'The court orders that:

1. The applications for a Residence Order and the return of the children to the Applicant's care be listed at York County Court'.

Rose was shaking and felt sick; she read further down and the date was for Monday and it was Friday afternoon – 'feck' she said out loud and thought it was bloody good luck she was waiting in a solicitor's office for an appointment.

Rose was reading the document over and over again as she couldn't understand the legal jargon that it contained and eventually a very tall, slim brunette business-like woman with black round glasses at the end of her nose looked down at her paperwork and called Rose's name. Rose felt that she was at school and had been called into the headmaster's office. Again she prepared to feel shameful of why she was there.

Her solicitor shook her hand and invited her to sit down alongside, introducing herself. "Hi, I'm Jessica White and I'm the

Managing Director of Smiths' Solicitors. You're here for a divorce, is that correct?" She barely even looked at Rose, but down at the form she had filled in. Rose felt like she was a box on a conveyer belt and it was getting checked off for delivery.

Rose had sat down as she was invited to and took a deep breath thinking it was going to take a lot to explain but she started with the most concerning factor and that she had just received an email. Rose showed it to Jessica on her iPhone.

Jessica White shook her head. "Ok, so the divorce is going to have to wait because you're in court on Monday and it's Friday today. We are going to have to get a witness statement together now and I will have to get hold of a solicitor in York to attend this. It's going to be £500 before VAT and I would suggest you don't go unrepresented to this court case."

Rose immediately said 'shit' and she saw Jessica White's eyebrows raise and her eyes glance at Rose over her spectacles.

"Erm, sorry....ok, we will do that. How do I pay?" And, Jessica explained that a card payment would suffice and it needed to be paid before 4pm today. She would have to find a solicitor in York and give them all the notes.

Rose knew she had to say yes, and then sort it out by doing a mass phone call to everyone. This was a matter of keeping the children with her or losing them to Darren.

Jessica White continued, "Ok, so let's sort this meeting out first; I'm going to need to know everything! Every reason as to why you should have the children stay with you and why he should not."

Rose was thinking to herself how thankful she was that she was incredibly organised and she had a file with all the evidence she had been collecting since a few weeks before Darren threw her out. Rose had a copy of the discharge letter from the hospital regarding Harrison which she believed would be the biggest piece of evidence out of everything Rose had collated. Rose had accumulated photos of the children's deterioration over the last few weeks of them being in sole care of Darren which included Harrison's conjunctivitis, very raw nappy rash, dirty soiled clothes, and a mouldy dummy. She even had voice recordings from when Rose was still living with Darren and his threats to her; she had her texts and email screenshots and everything that would certainly help her case. Rose also mentioned that she had called the local authorities as she was worried about the children's welfare and she had had a lot of contact with the police and had reference numbers with dates.

It was like a scene from a television crime show, with Rose pushing all of the material towards Jessica on the table. When Rose saw it all, it looked more like it was an obsession of convicting a criminal and said to Jessica, "I have been on my own for a few weeks and it's all I've thought about. Tim and I started to collate everything that we thought could help and it's really important to me because he has stolen the last 6 years of my life."

After an hour of discussing the main factors and Jessica White taking what she believed would be relevant evidence to put towards Rose's statement, there was the questioning. Jessica treated Rose like it was an interrogation challenging different aspects of what Rose said and the relationship: why it took her so long to leave him, why the police weren't involved sooner, why did he throw her out, why, why, why, why, and WHY!!!

After the meeting, Rose had the most outrageous pounding headache from spending an hour justifying her side of the story. Rose rang Tim from the waiting room and explained in a panicky rush what was going on and what needed to be done. Tim asked her to meet him outside the solicitor's and he would meet her in the car with the children.

Rose explained to the secretary that she would be back before 4pm to pay the balance and she was surprised at herself that she was somewhat convincing. Rose didn't know how on earth she was going to get this money but there had to be a way.

Rose waited outside the solicitor's office in the mild air. She was hunched over, looking down at the ground and feeling in need of a hug. A few tears dropped to the ground. Rose was yet again in a Dene when Tim pulled up in the lay-by nearest to her. He stepped out and helped her into the car as if she had sprained an ankle and was unable to walk. Rose looked up and gave a slight smile at him in thanks and sat in the passenger seat of the car feeling sorry for herself.

Tim stroked her face and gave her a kiss on the cheek and said, "You stay here with the kids and I'll go and have a word with the receptionist, ok?" Rose just nodded in the fog she was in; her mind was elsewhere and she felt she was back to square one. She couldn't be free just yet, she was still under his control.

Tim left the car and walked into the office building, Rose

looked back at her children. The pain swept over her in full force; she had only just gotten them back and she didn't want to lose them to Darren. She knew it was best if they were to live with her. She had been a full-time mum since the day Millie-Rose was born.

Before she knew it, Tim was back and he got in the car stating, "All sorted, nothing for you to worry about."

Rose was confused but didn't have the energy to question him. Instead she gave him a kiss on the cheek and said, "Let's get home before Harrison gets upset with his chest."

Tim drove them home wanting to take all the worries away from Rose. He knew the hardest part wasn't bringing the kids to her hometown but to fight Darren in court and justify why he shouldn't have them.

That afternoon was quite pleasant. Rose had needed to send a couple of emails back to the solicitor and confirm the statement was correct and she had also managed to arrange for her Auntie Lucy to babysit whilst they went to court.

For the first time they spent the afternoon playing hide and seek, making dens and colouring with the kids and for some reason it ended up in a tickle fight which meant Rose found out that Tim was extremely ticklish (especially on his feet) and the kids and her enjoyed watching him in fits of laughter until Tim shouted out, "Don't do anymore don't...I'm going to..." Too late he let out a huge pump... but everyone laughed! Rose felt it was lovely to be normal for a little while and put everything to the back of their heads. Everyone needs some time out from reality once in a while, wouldn't it be good if there was an on and off switch?

It was soon the evening to a long weekend and Tim had organised a babysitter for the children so that they could go out for a meal. He wanted to give Rose some distraction and time out from worrying; he thought when the good is going good, then keep rolling with it. They enjoyed a local cuisine of Dutch pancakes with savoury and sweet toppings, something they both hadn't tried before. Tim noticed Rose wasn't really with him through the meal and he tried to talk about other things and 'get to know' Rose a bit more, like a proper date. Tim was really understanding and supportive and the more they spent time together the more Rose was opening up to him and building her trust and ability to lean on him for that support. It was going to take a long time to feel normal and it would never truly heal, but day by day and step by step Tim had promised to be there for her and the kids. Rose couldn't get all the memories out of her head, specifically those before she was thrown out into the street.

* * *

It was two weeks before Darren had decided to throw me out for good; I had already been enduring the intimidating feel of Darren's presence (that's all it took these days). Darren and I had been separated for a couple of months and since then Darren had started to wake me up in the middle of the night in the attempt to 'sort the problem out' and clearly he knew I would be confused and disorientated to what was going on.

I was a deep sleeper and having two young children, I was exhausted. I had been sleeping on the sofa downstairs for the first month and eventually Darren said he should sleep on the sofa although he suggested first that we sleep next to each other and that I shouldn't be so stupid.

I got back into the marital bed without Darren, of course. He was on the sofa (about time I thought), at least I would get some good rest. That's when each night Darren started to wake me up again trying to 'get things sorted'. I was confused, as I had been every other time, and was adamant to leave it. I was happy with the way things were going, pleased with the decision that I had regained a little control for once.

After a week, I ended up waking up next to Darren himself. He had started climbing into the bed whilst I was asleep; this freaked me out and I resorted back to the sofa. I had started to become very ill with the lack of sleep and the stress of the situation. I was having severe headaches and was vomiting although I didn't think it was a bad thing because in the last two months I had lost 1 1/2 stone. I was very good at getting on with everything despite all that was going on. I only had Tim to confide in as I knew it would take the energy out of me if I confided in friends or family and I couldn't be dealing with their opinions.

Darren had become more intimidating and was picking arguments with everyone. The pressure was sky high and I had become numb to what he was saying to me: 'you're useless, you'll regret this for the rest of your life, no one would have you because you're a nut case. I'll tell the courts you have bi-polar, you're a slut, you're a bad mum, the kids would be better off without you. I'll tell them you've had three different counsellors', the threats went on and on.

Alongside his threatening stare and constant demands, I realised I was winning. I was able to see Tim and cry on his shoulder and have the time out to recharge and prepare for another blank expression.

I didn't quite expect what would happen next but Darren had always placed mild threats alongside his manipulation and this time he was threatening for money. "I want £200 by next week or I'll be throwing you out."

Tim reassured me and said that he was bluffing but there was something about this that didn't sound as if he was. I had explained I had no money, in fact reminded him that I was in debt because of him. I knew I couldn't get out of this situation easily or peacefully. I was like a robot in his company now, a blank expression. It was like Darren had wiped out my identity over the years. I already watched who I spoke to, where I went, what I did because of his jealousy and self-esteem issues. I used to pity him.

Then the week passed and Darren made a point of it, "Tomorrow, if I don't have the £200, you are out." Was he bluffing like Tim had said? And then a statement came that I wasn't expecting,

"Believe you me, Rose... I can be a right nasty bastard even more than I have ever been! Do you understand that?"

I simply smiled back at him, the first time I was unable to be robotic and it was as if someone had switched my feelings and emotions back on. I was smiling out loud in my head and couldn't believe it. I was always wondering if Darren knew what he was doing to me and I had strived to get through it thinking he hadn't a clue. Despite the numerous attempts to get him to agree to see a couple's counsellor, he had not shown up and had told me everything was my fault and there would be no problems if I fixed the way I was. I spent a year of going each week to counselling myself; I had believed it was my fault and had told my friends that I was sorting it out.

It wasn't me though and the three counsellors I had gone to all said that I needed to have couple's counselling because all my problems were to do with HIM! This moment ticked another box in my head and the day eventually came when he threw me out but at least, at long last, I knew in my head that the pieces did fit together. It was like a huge epiphany, and I knew that one day my life would get sorted without him in it.

CHAPTER TEN

The weekend seemed to be never-ending for Rose and Tim felt the same as he watched Rose stuck in an emotional turmoil. Rose was exhausted from the lack of sleep and every time she fell into a sleep it was a very deep sleep and full of nightmares about the different possible outcomes of the court hearing.

Rose's mind was racing with memories and again she was zoned out in her white noise. Despite Rose and Tim going out with the children each day, Rose was on auto pilot and would come back to reality when spotting different things that reminded her of her life with Darren or when Tim managed to drag her out of the trance and get her attention.

Tim had driven Rose and the kids out to a Designer Outlet for the day which wasn't that far from Liverpool. Tim thought it would be beneficial for a change of scenery. It was a cold crisp day and they had wrapped up warm. It was all exciting for Millie-Rose and Harrison because they had never been before; they loved to go on adventures and see new places. Once Tim had parked up they first headed over to the outdoor play area for the kids. They absolutely loved going on the climbing frame and rushing down the slide.

Rose and Tim stood and watched them, "They're really good kids, you know?" Tim started a conversation with Rose. Rose smiled at Tim and leant to the side for Tim to put his arm around her (and keep her warm).

"Thank you," Rose said quietly.

"I'm not just saying it you know, you've done a fab job with them." Tim wanted her to see that someone had recognised her as a mummy.

"If I was a good mum and if I had have done a good job then I would have left him sooner and not put them through all this."

Rose felt disappointed with herself. Tim was just about to respond when Rose spoke again, "I don't understand why you're even with me and doing this because surely you wouldn't want to be with someone like me, a failure, a disappointment. I mean, what do your parents think because I know what I would be thinking if it was one of my children and them giving up everything to help someone with two children in a very complicated situation."

Tim looked at Rose and his eyes spoke to her a disappointment that she would even think that. "My parents support me and the decisions I make, no matter what my decisions are."

And Rose interrupted, "That doesn't mean that they agree or like your decision, though."

Tim looked down at Rose through his eyebrows and frowned, "You can't fight me on everything Rose, why are you worried about that anyway?"

Rose quickly replied, "Because Tim, you mean something to me and I care about what they think...because I want them to like me."

Tim let out a light sigh, "Let them help and as they do, they will get to know you and they will not just like you but they will love you, because you're caring, creative, funny, loving and of course you have a good head on your shoulders."

Rose elbowed Tim bashfully and shrugged off the compliment. "You're just saying that."

Tim wasn't going to listen to Rose and said, "You may not accept my opinion but it's still myyyy opinion! You're always unaccepting of anything nice I say about you and I want to change that; I want you to see yourself the way I do."

Rose gave Tim a peck on the cheek and they continued to watch Millie-Rose and Harrison who were starting to compete with each other on who could climb the highest on the frame and Rose was getting concerned as she watched Harrison almost reach the top. She ran over and hovered her hand below his bottom just in case he lost his balance.

After a fun half an hour, they all set off around the shops. Rose loved to window shop and walk around looking at things she wanted to buy. Tim had told Rose that he was going to treat her as she and the kids needed some new clothes since they had left Darren's with hardly anything. Tim directed them to Next which had a clearance on, thankfully it wasn't that busy for a Saturday. The clearance racks hit them as soon as they walked in and Rose went hunting through the selection for the children; she thought there were some really nice clothes but she would never pay the price for them, even if they were reduced.

"They've got plenty for the kids, haven't they?" Tim smiled and gestured to the selection.

"Yes they do, but I would never pay these prices, Tim." Rose was trying to usher everyone back out the door. Tim insisted they stay and told Millie-Rose to have a look at whatever clothes she would like and assisted her and Harrison to choose.

"Now, you go and pick whatever you want," he directed to Rose. Rose walked over to the women's clothes rack and looked through the selection, muttering to herself: 'too small…. too low cut… too slim fit…too big… too fancy…too expensive…' There was nothing that would take to her taste but she made an effort to carry on looking. Rose hated shopping for clothes for herself simply because she hadn't done it in over a year and didn't spend money on herself, it all went on her children and what they needed and wanted.

* * *

It was years into my relationship with Darren and I had lost friends, hardly ever saw my family and just before the business idea came up in my mind, I had lost all interest in looking after my appearance. Darren had always put pressure on me about my weight and how I looked. After Harrison, he was conscious of me getting back to my slim self. He had even referenced me one day and said I had more roll-backs than Asda! To be honest I thought this was a little harsh because if you saw a photo of me then I wasn't fat at all; I was half a stone over the average weight for my height and age and that did class me as overweight medically but looking at me you wouldn't have been able to tell (probably because it's all packed into my peachy bum behind me).

Because he had said I needed to lose weight and kept on calling me different names and 'casually' dropping it into the conversation and even turned his nose up when seeing me half naked; well, I basically turned to my one vice and that's chocolate. I didn't want to lose the weight because he had made me feel horrible and me being an emotional eater it just didn't get me anywhere. I was too tired to be concerned. Darren ended up having control of nearly every aspect of my life; he was a puppet master and my strings were triple knotted to the controls; I was his dummy.

Looking back, I hadn't noticed that it was so invasive and I was manipulated into believing that this was normal. I remember one day I had been to a bank meeting regarding my debt and had been gone an hour; of course Darren wasn't with me but he had come into town because my life had become so controlled that he wouldn't let me go anywhere alone anymore.

Darren met me after my meeting and he had a big bag of Primark clothes which is where I loved to shop because I was on a tight budget and their children's selection was just fantastic. I often got my pyjamas and coats from there. Anyway, he passed it to me and I guess at the time I thought it was a nice gesture but he had bought me some tops, a pair of shoes and a summer jacket. He knew not to buy any trousers or jeans because I have to try on every pair I buy due to the shape of my bottom, in fact when the J-Lo range of jeans were out, they worked wonders. I thanked Darren and to be honest I did like the clothes. I could see a lovely vest top that would clearly hide my mummy tummy and I smiled and even said it would look nice on me.

I remember Darren then informing me, "Well… I didn't really know what to buy you so I asked the woman in the shop and said what clothes would be good for my wife, she has a podgy tummy and so she wants to hide it."

I swore at him (in my head of course) and because I had trained myself, I let the comment pass my head and I put it into a locked box. I knew he was ashamed to be next to me and he didn't want to be seen with me and my podge. To be honest, I didn't even know he saw it because when we had sex I would keep my top on and keep the light off so he couldn't see my body, the body he would look at in disgust.

It was particularly funny that once he had called a day on the relationship that I lost the weight in no time and had bought some new clothes and I looked absolutely fabulous and the men seemed to be interested. I felt amazing and it was for me – not him! I was getting the old fun me back and re-gaining my identity.

* * *

Rose was fighting her crossed opinions and didn't know what was best and what she could wear now she was with Tim.

Tim came over with Millie-Rose who was carrying a pile of clothes that she could barely see over the top. "Look Mummy, look Mummy!!!" She was so excited to show Rose what she had chosen. Harrison wanted to jump out of Tim's arms to Rose and was pointing to the shopping carrier which was full of clothes for Harrison.

"We needed another shopping basket," Tim giggled. "They loved deciding on what they wanted," and he had this huge smile on his face with the children all beaming at her, and then Tim realised Rose had nothing, not one item, and Tim looked puzzled.

"I can't find anything," and again before Tim could jump the gun, Rose raised her eyebrows, "and…I thought we could look another day as I'm feeling rather tired and not too well anyway." Rose didn't want to worry anyone and was enjoying the time with Tim and the kids. In fact, she was welling up because they had never looked so happy.

They carried on walking around the outlet and had gone into a few shops and Tim had bought some toys and activities for the children. Rose thought Tim was over-confident about the outcome of the upcoming court hearing. Rose was too polite to say anything and she was enjoying the pretence they were putting on for the children.

They both headed into Starbucks with the children under Tim's direction; for Rose it was like a glamorous afternoon out compared to the years of hard up for money with Darren. Rose didn't particularly want to go into Starbucks because of the memories that came back to haunt her, even the little one's nagged at her.

* * *

It was a wet day and Darren and I had reached for cover in Starbucks as we were out at the bank to open a savings account for Millie-Rose; she was just two months old. Starbucks was naturally dark as it was in their design but today it was even darker due to the miserable weather. Millie-Rose didn't like it at all. As soon as we went to the counter for a coffee she woke up and started to stir, perhaps she couldn't adjust to the light. I thought she was just waking up and ready for some milk so I went to find a place to sit and the window seemed appealing because I needed some light to see what I was doing. I attempted to get Millie-Rose out and onto my boob but she wasn't having any of it, she really wasn't happy; she burst out screaming (she had figured out what her lungs were, clearly).

Darren, the staff and everyone in Starbucks looked directly at me as if to see if I'd harmed my beautiful baby. But no, all they saw was me attempting to get her onto my boob and it wasn't a pretty sight as I was getting rather stressed out and my hair was getting in my way. It looked like I was rugby tackling her. Millie-Rose was clearly not going to latch on and a few passers-by had gained a flash of my tit and my struggling girl refusing to have my nipple put in her mouth. I put her over my shoulder and started to rock her, "Shhhhhhh it's ok, sshhhhhh," I said softly.

Darren made his way over with his cappuccino and my large caramel latte. "That's it Rose, show everyone your boob!" he snapped and then muttered under his breath, "this is exactly why she should have a bottle."

I couldn't be bothered to give him the satisfaction of responding. I had just struggled to sort Millie out and was rather thirsty. "She will have a bottle once I can start building up my breast milk to store."

Darren wasn't impressed with my comment. "That's not what I meant and you know it," his reply was unsupportive. I felt good that I was sticking to my ground on this one because I wanted to feed Millie-Rose myself. It was a lovely thing to do and it helped me bond with her.

"I can't do anything to help because I can't feed her." I rolled my eyes back as I'd heard it all before and he was still persistent on going over it again and reeling off his opinion.

"I'm not going to get into it again but I think babies need their nappies changing and bathing and some hugs and burping..." I could get away with being sarcastic in public.

"I would bond better if I could feed her a bottle." I just let him rant on yet again at me about it and I planned not to go to Starbucks again because Millie-Rose seemed to kick up a fuss plus it was another place tainted with something negative, even the small negatives were a big deal because that's what they were to him.

* * *

Tim had managed to make Rose's experience of Starbucks a nicer time. He was feeling good by treating her and the kids to hot chocolates with cream and marshmallows and a selection of cakes. Rose was on cloud nine but in a haze still with the court case at the back of her mind. She was watching Tim and the children make milk moustaches and giggled along with them. Tim encouraged Millie-Rose and Harrison to put the cream on Rose's nose and they had a lot of fun together. Rose kept thinking what life would have been like if she had met Tim before Darren and skipped him altogether but she couldn't forget how wonderful her two children were and how they were a blessing.

After a fun afternoon out, they went back home; Millie-Rose and Harrison had fallen asleep in the back of the car and both Tim and Rose scooped them out of their car seats carefully, so as not to wake them, and managed to tuck them into bed.

Once the kids were settled in bed, Tim started to organise the shopping which Rose thought was rather peculiar. Rose offered to help but Tim turned around to face her and smiled and said, "I was looking for this," and he handed over a Pandora gift bag.

Rose had wondered how on earth Tim had managed to slip that past her and felt unsure about accepting the gift. Tim passed it to her all excited but cool and suave with his broad shoulders looking all handsome. She loved him holding her and belonging in his arms. Tim placed the gift into her hand and instructed her, "Don't think about it and don't fight it; just open it."

Rose wasn't going to refuse but still felt like she couldn't accept it; she wasn't used to getting gifts and felt that she didn't deserve it. Rose carefully pulled the salmon pink ribbon bow and opened the gift bag to see a Pandora gift box eagerly awaiting her to open it. Rose had started to become all nervous and carefully slipped off the sleeve surrounding the box and prized the box open. Rose was so happy and smiled a wide smile which happened to be the biggest smile she had given in years. Gleaming up at her was a Pandora purple leather bracelet with one single charm, the charm was a surrounded with tiny silver hearts with an accent golden heart.

Tim then explained to Rose, "I chose the bracelet because this is the start of your new life and I am going to buy you a new charm for each step or achievement you take now that you're free. The first charm is there to remind you of the love you have shined out to me and now you're the only woman I will love and I'm going to be with you every step in your new life."

Rose was overwhelmed with love for Tim; tears filled her eyes and she actually swooned while Tim held her face and leant in to kiss her. Rose soon fell into Tim's kiss and had shivers run down her spine. Her right hand sneakily slipped down and she gently groped his bottom and Tim returned the gesture. Soon they were kissing hard and attempting to work their way through the living room and through the kitchen to get up the stairs. Rose and Tim were lost in the moment and were giggling along the way, a trail of clothes had begun to follow them and Rose had never seen Tim this manly or horny; it turned her on even more. Rose took off his shirt to reveal a well-toned slender body. She ran her hands down his chest and cheekily felt his erection. Tim let out a sexy grunt and pulled her close into his arms. Tim sucked her neck and pushed her against the fridge which slammed against the wall; he put his arms either side of her and kissed her but Rose unexpectedly felt the urge to break free from being trapped and suddenly a gross memory took over her.

CHAPTER ELEVEN

I couldn't cope anymore, Den had pushed me and pushed me and spent the last two weeks winding me up. I was sleep deprived and I couldn't think straight. I was meant to be meeting up with my friend who had recently had a baby and I had met her at a baby group. The plan was for me to go over and visit her at the hospital as we had become rather close. Darren had been grumbling all day about it as he knew he would have to look after the children whilst I visited her. I had to ask his permission prior. It was almost time for me to go so I nipped up to the bedroom to get the gift I had put away for her.

Darren followed me up the stairs, "You're really going to go then?" he said rather softly but in a sly way. I took an inward large sigh and really couldn't be bothered to go through another battle with him. He had already been at it all day, making me think it was ok then 'pretending' it wasn't. I knew from this moment I wasn't going to be seeing my friend and her new baby but yet I still tried to make the attempt.

"Yes of course, just like we had planned," and I didn't even glance his way.

Darren had come over to me and gave my bum a squeeze as I tried to reach in the wardrobe for the gift, "I'll miss you; I just want to kiss you and feel your arseeee." He was trying to 'get me going' which he did not.

"Well, I'm only going to be out an hour so you'll just want me more when I get back." I was looking forward to being out for an hour.

"Are the kids fed and watered?" he asked. I knew where this was going too (that he can't look after them and that they would be without if I'm not there).

I was trying to tug a gift out of the wardrobe but Darren kept on putting me off with his wandering hands that tickled me and it wasn't going down well. I felt like it was an invasion of my personal space and in the end I snapped at him, "Look can't you see I'm struggling and I cannot concentrate with you doing that?"

I shouldn't have said it because he thoroughly enjoyed responding, "Well, if you think you are going to talk to me like that then you've got another thing coming. I'm going to my mum's."

It was like he knew what he was doing and wanted to push me so he had a reason to leave me hanging and spoil my plans and I knew what he wanted and that was for me to beg him, beg him so I could go.

"Who's going to have the kids, then?" I asked thinking I could quiz him instead.

"Well you, of course, that's a daft question!" And instead of fighting it this time I thought I would take them and I'd ring round a few friends to have them (I was really hoping it would call his bluff).

I climbed up using the bed to aid me and he grabbed my arm, smiled and whispered in my ear, "I'm just joking, you silly cow," (maybe it had worked, I thought).

"Ok well, I need to get going so could you help me get this damn present, I don't know what it's stuck on?" I ignored the name calling (little old robot me) and flicked my long hair out of the way to gasp for some air.

"Of course, my love!" he said in a sly way yet again and he pulled out the gift like I had loosened a jar lid and he opened it.

"Typical, eh?" I said and started to head out of the bedroom.

Darren stopped me in my tracks, "When are you giving her the present then?" I just had no clue what was going on at this point, he had completely confused me.

"Well, I'm going now, aren't I?" and Darren laughed like it was a hilarious joke.

"You IDIOT!!! Didn't you hear? I'm going to my mum's."

Why won't he just make up his mind. Why is he playing these games? I wasn't going to give him the satisfaction, "Oh, ok sorry…I'll take the kids with me then," and smiled politely and tried to get past him.

Darren interrupted, "I think you've lost your keys," and he held them up and dangled them from the tip of his finger rather camp like.

I couldn't cope with it any longer. I was so stressed out and exhausted, I completely flipped and I started kicking and hitting the new wooden bed I had just bought.

He looked at me with disgust on his face, like I was the most vile thing he had ever seen and said with a stuck up nose, "Oh my God…you're insane…who would want to be with you…you've lost the plot."

I stopped hitting and kicking the bed and shot my head at him and screamed as if I was going to charge at him but got down to the floor and banged my head three times on the floor. To be honest, that moment was really blurry and looking back I WAS insane and I DID lose the plot but he had driven me to this state; he had been grooming me to have an argument or flare up.

It was always the same cycle and I knew what he was doing to me, and no matter how hard I tried to ignore it, it got to me. I couldn't do anything right. My nose had started to run as I had started to cry and my head was pounding. I got myself together rather quickly, marched down the stairs and got the kids into the car and simply drove away. All he wanted was for me not to go and see my friend and he won! I sat in the car bawling my eyes out and considered taking myself to A&E. I had a huge lump on my head from where I had hurt it. The worst thing was, how would I explain it because he didn't do it physically to me. I think he wanted to but he soon saw that he could do it to me without using his own energy and watch me mentally break down.

Little things became huge deals and they were important because they were the things that were keeping me a real person and not a drone. I had some time away from him with the children and had a walk round a country park, thankfully the rain stayed away. I needed to have some fresh air and I felt very dizzy after hurting myself so bad. I looked in the rear view mirror and saw a lump the size of a golf ball. I did feel a bit better after a walk, although watching Millie-Rose help Harrison go on a 'bear hunt' in the woods was just so cute and made me tearful. They were amazingly well behaved children and they deserved so much more.

Again, I had this huge guilt hang over me like a lead balloon, I could feel it heavy in the pit of my stomach. Was it too much to ask? Why couldn't Darren just be normal? I would have carried on loving him like any normal relationship. I knew I would have to go back yet again and face him and he would feel full and fed from me, because that's what I did; I slipped up and I lashed out and I fed him what he wanted to see, he wanted to see me lose it.

Each time he would wind me up a little more, apply more pressure, push the button harder, tighten the collar around my neck. After a couple of hours of crying in the fresh air I went to face him; I built up what was left of my energy and I went back to where he was likely waiting to punish me for my behaviour. He would want me to plead for him to keep me and apologise. I was a master of this cycle and I knew what to expect next.

I went home despite knowing this and I knew he was there waiting for me. I'd like to say he was like a puppy waiting for its owner to come home but it was more like a Rottweiler that hadn't been fed for days.

He went straight for me with his tone of voice and pathetic attempt of sarcasm. The kids didn't pick up on it of course. He pretty much talked at me for the rest of the day wondering where I had been, why I hadn't told him, was I with another man; it was the same old record being played over and over again. I couldn't take another interrogation and I spent the afternoon with the white noise of the world, my mind giving a loud flat-line buzz to cover up his nasty accusations and words that scarred.

The children went to bed and it was as if they knew what was going on because they would settle down fast on days like these. On a quiet day they would want for me a lot. It seemed to me that they were in tune with the situation and they needed to go to bed to be able to shut down and not be exposed to the cruel intentions. It made me worry that they would grow up like this and be desensitised to this relationship and follow suit.

I gave them both a kiss on the cheek. I used to hate putting the children to bed on days like these because he used to think that they couldn't hear; he used to think they would zone off and not remember. He used this time to crank it up to top gear and make me suffer and watch me squirm. I wish you could have seen me; I was really good at zoning out. It was like a brainwashed glaze over my eyes would be turned on but the problem was, I couldn't go on for hours and he had already stuck the knife in over and over again for several.

In the end it would always be something stupid that I would react to and tonight it started with a comment, "This is why you shouldn't deprive me, I haven't had it for a couple of weeks now and you can see I'm frustrated." Darren wasn't directing it at me, he was muttering this under his breath but he knew I would hear and it was his 'clever' way of bringing me out of this trance and I did. My blood was boiling and my breathing became heavy.

Darren carried on, "I mean we are meant to be married, but that doesn't account for anything these days." My heart was starting to race. "Just to think all my mates are getting it."

And that was it, the twig was firmly broken in half. I jumped up off the sofa to which I had been glued to, a mould from my body and wanting to keep me there. I went off into the kitchen and started to wash the pots, loudly. I was banging away at putting them down and sighing and I had to mutter under my breath.

Darren gave it just the right amount of time as usual and then followed me in like a lost sheep, "How dare you walk out on me when I am talking to you."

I didn't care about my reply anymore and this is what got me into more trouble, "Talking AT me, more like." I shoved it back to him under my breath thinking two can play at that game.

"Sorry, WHAT did you say?" he said disgusted. "I didn't quite hear that, do you want to say it to my face?"

I thought in my head how childish this was and I didn't realise we were in school. I inadvertently giggled because he couldn't hear my thoughts at least. I carried on washing the pots and went to get the tea towel off the side of the counter near him as if he was invisible but he grabbed my wrist and repeated himself to me.

"Sorry..." and took a long pause, "...what... did... you... say.... to me?"

My heart was now out of my chest; I couldn't quite hear him because the beating of my heart was echoing in my ears; was he going to hit me? I daren't struggle. He yanked me forward and put his mouth close to my ear and whispered loudly, "Do I need to ask again?"

I held my breath so he couldn't hear the shaking in it, I didn't want him to know he was winning. He manned up to me like he was a bully at high school and I was the school geek and pushed me against the kitchen cupboards. I could see the knife block and I wanted to grab the biggest one and sink it into him; was it wrong that I often thought of different ways to kill him but ideally get away with it (I had thought of poisoning, a hit man). I was too scared to reach for it in case he got there first and I kicked him hard in the chin which I wasn't expecting. I ran out of the house and ran away. I knew if I let him cool off, or should I say if I cooled off and had a breather (half time break) then I could come back and reset my settings.

When I got back from a brisk ten-minute walk, I was ready for the next round. Everything seemed calm and Darren came to me and said, "I think it's best for me if we call it a day." Fireworks went off in my head. I had been waiting for him to call it off and set me free and he went on to say, "So I think you need to go hunting for your own place to live; the kids can see you one day a week," and the fireworks stopped. I did everything for the kids, if he ever did anything he would make it a huge issue and it would result in the children being upset and wanting me.

I thought about this strategically and I simply said, "Well, we can talk about all that another day because I'm tired and I need to go to sleep," and I headed upstairs.

Darren stopped me, "Where do you think you're going?" I looked at him puzzled, "Where am I going to sleep?"

I just didn't argue and I got my things from the bedroom to where he had followed me. "Why are you ignoring me? I'm sleeping in here." He couldn't wait to see what I was doing and I picked up my pillow and stuff and went downstairs to sleep on the sofa. To be honest I was excited about the end but I knew it wasn't really the end for him, it was just another way of trying to scare me. What he really wanted was for me to beg him to stay with me but I had gotten past that point. I wasn't a blow up doll that he could use for sex anymore. There would be no more crying in the loo after, there would be no more waking up in the middle of the night because he had decided to have sex with me whilst I was asleep, there would be no showering to get his smell off me.

* * *

Rose was breathing fast and shallow and had started to panic. Tim was shaking her, "Rose, Rose, is everything ok?" Rose was again in a familiar haze and not knowing what was going on, she tried to catch her breath. Tim grabbed a glass of water and held it in her hand with her. "Come on, take a drink of this, you need to calm down." Tim was worried about Rose and wanted to help, Rose took a tiny sip but she was still tuned into what she had remembered and panted more, slid down to the floor and hid in her arms. Tim put his arms round her and just hugged her. Rose rocked back and forth crying in a ball in his arms.

Half an hour later, Tim had managed to assist Rose to the living-room couch and Rose had caught her breath back a little but was still upset.

"I'm so sorry," Rose started to apologise, "I... I... I feel so stupid."

"Stop it and don't tell me anything unless you want to."

"You must think... you must think... I'm a nut case," Rose was sobbing as she was making herself more upset about what she believed Tim would be thinking.

"You know whatever it is, I'm here and I don't think you're a nut case, I just want to help you, we don't have to do anything until you're ready."

Rose sobbed more, "I wanted to, I was enjoying every minute of it….. it was just…. just…. that you did something…"

"What did I do? Because I won't ever do it again. The last thing I want to do is hurt or upset you."

Rose grabbed Tim's neck and pulled him in for a hug. "I don't want to spoil anything; I'm falling for you."

Tim smiled and said, "You never have to worry about spoiling us because I'm in love with you and we can get through anything. I believe in us." Rose pined for Tim and he said, "Don't you remember? I was there right from when I met you."

* * *

I couldn't go to sleep on that sofa. I decided to go on my iPhone and chat to a few people. Tim was new on the scene as I had met him at a speed networking event. I can't deny there wasn't chemistry but he didn't really know what situation I was in. Anyway, he seemed to be the one I could chat to and it was fantastic as he was a new business contact so I would talk about business related stuff; we swapped some great contacts despite it being late at night. Tim and I seemed to be getting to know each other through the businesses. He would strategically go into a personal conversation and ask me things and add in that I looked pretty on the photo I recently shared. Tim knew that online networking was becoming my new life-saver and if I hadn't have had the business then I wouldn't have a focus and it became the thing I used to switch off. If it wasn't for The Perfect Gift Co, then I wouldn't be in this position.

I knew that I could cope with Darren's behaviour over the coming weeks with the separation because I could lock myself up in the dining room on an evening and get on with my orders and if I managed to get them sorted then I would just work on new ideas. I could do some online networking which gave me a great excuse to talk to Tim and my current friends and connections who were supporting me. I would have never thought that I would be so excited to be working and it was all thanks to the children; they gave me the ideas.

I kept thinking on where I started just a few months ago – Harrison had given me the idea. It was hard to have my handbag, changing bag a toddler and then a baby; it was simply too much to carry and I started to put my nappies and wipes loosely in my oversized handbag which wasn't really convenient so one day I sewed a nappy and wipes' case with some Velcro to seal it. I went along to baby groups and everyone wanted to buy one and thus the business was born. It was one of the best things that had ever happened to me.

Tim was impressed and saw that it developed into handmade purses and even handbags that were user friendly for mums. Thankfully, Tim was a connection to keep close because he ran a business called Marketing 4 U and specialised in social media marketing. It was impressive as he had been in business for 8 years and had employees so I felt privileged to even be talking to him. I felt completely out of his league in the business world, never mind the personal world. Tim chatted away to me until around 2am. He had no idea what was going on in my life and it felt so nice to forget about it all and chat about the business and he took my mind off the personal struggles I was having.

* * *

Rose did remember and she remembered how Tim changed her way of thinking from the moment he stepped into her life; he helped her gain a different focus and it started as her business and him giving her the confidence which made her strive to gain more success. "You will never know... you will never know exactly what you saved me from."

Tim responded, "I don't need to know and all that you need to know now is that you're safe with me and I will look after you."

That's all Rose ever wanted from a family: a husband to protect and look after her. Darren had abused all aspects of that and Tim was picking up the pieces. Tim was making a dream a reality.

CHAPTER TWELVE

The court day had finally arrived and Rose woke up feeling jet-lagged; she had hardly slept a wink. She was encouraged to have some breakfast by Tim. She turned her nose up at it but welcomed a well-known hug in a mug of tea (nothing could beat a Twinings Breakfast tea). Tim left Rose to get ready and thought it was best not to interfere and give her some space.

Rose looked like a headless chicken running backwards and forwards from the bathroom to the bedroom and then the mirror on the top of the landing. In the end, it took a quarter of the time it normally took Rose to get looking lovely, which meant there was a lot of dead time to watch the clock and feel more sick about D-day.

Rose spent the morning on her iPhone doing some chatting with close friends and some business networking; the distraction didn't work for her though because time seemed to have stopped completely and she couldn't get her mind off the possible outcomes of the court hearing which was approaching ever so slowly.

Rose went for a lie-down and put the radio on, something she rarely got the chance to do and thought now was as good of a time as any. Rose couldn't believe what she was hearing when she switched it on, 'Would it make you feel better to watch me while I bleed'. Rose's ears pricked up and she soaked up the lyrics that were being sung; she couldn't believe how she could relate to this song. 'You can take everything I have…go on and try to tear me down'. Rose's heart was racing and a wash of anger, upset, hatred, shame and embarrassment came over her. 'How did he get away with this? Why was I so naïve'? she thought.

Rose shazammed the song and it was Ellie Goulding's Skyscraper and in no time at all Rose downloaded it onto her iPhone and played it a couple more times to herself. It seemed to get her blood pumped and give her the huge determination she needed to finally fight for what was right and not let Darren treat her like a piece of shit on the end of his shoe. Rose knew that this song was going to be something that would inspire her to keep going in the tough times to come and she knew she couldn't forget what Darren had done to her; this would certainly help her to remember what he put her through.

The time had finally come to get in the car and set off; they were going to make very good time and get there early. Rose wanted to arrive before Darren. The journey to the court seemed like it took triple the length of time it normally did although Tim's dad was driving and he was always a calm driver. She was getting sick of being frozen in time.

Rose was picking away at a tissue and made a mess on the car seat with tiny shreds now everywhere. Rose wasn't concerned about any mess she was making. It was as if she couldn't hear anyone or anything around her but her thoughts spotlighted to this next event. When they arrived, they parked up and walked in, first through the security section which beeped as soon as Rose went through and it gave her a little jump. She had to be examined with the security wand instead. Rose felt shook up by it as for some reason she hadn't expected this at a county court and felt like a criminal instantly; again the shame washed over her with the fact that she was even in a court house.

When she walked through the doors to the waiting room, her friend was waiting to greet her. Rose had called a friend to attend with her because she wanted another support person and didn't know how many of Darren's family would be appearing today. Darren was nowhere to be seen but Rose's barrister was there waiting for her arrival.

The barrister summoned Tim and her into a side room to discuss the case. Rose was rather impressed with just how much the barrister knew and he had clearly done his homework (which the bill was reflecting). He was middle-aged and had Harry Potter-type glasses on with a nice business suit and spoke rather posh.

Rose's adrenalin was off the scale now and the barrister seemed to know what he was talking about so he went to check if Darren had arrived. He had arrived and surprisingly was on his own, which came as a shock to everyone. Tim's parents were still in the waiting room; Darren had never seen them before so he didn't know who they were.

The barrister went over to Darren and asked if he had seen the statement from Rose to which he said he hadn't as it was over the weekend. The barrister handed a copy to him as Darren was unrepresented and then he came back into the room. Tim's parents watched Darren read it and saw that he went bright red in a fluster and mouthed 'shit' under his breath. Darren hadn't expected Rose to disclose everything; perhaps he thought she wasn't strong enough to do it but Rose knew if it was about the children and where they should live then it had to be done with no holding back on what he had done to her.

She hoped that there would be no negative outcome from Darren and his family as a result of her speaking out. Rose was so protective of her two children. She knew she had to put her fears aside and she felt a lot better knowing Darren couldn't touch or say anything to her whilst in court which gave her the confidence to finally speak out. He couldn't hurt her now and Rose couldn't undo what was already done.

It felt like years had passed before their names were called and it was time to go into court. Rose's heart was beating so fast she couldn't feel the adrenalin rush. It was similar to a humming bird when their wings flap so fast that it makes a humming sound.

Rose sat down next to her barrister on the far side so she didn't have to sit next to Darren. She had totally missed the part of the conversation which told her what her barrister was actually called and she didn't care to know unless the outcome was in her favour.

The judge seemed rather intimidating to Rose. She looked at him and said to herself, 'this person is going to decide the fate of my children and where they should live; please be fair, please listen to me'. It dawned on her that her mother's instinct was taken away and that she had no control over protecting her children and what she thought would be best for them was now taken out of her hands and into the hands of the law.

The case started with the barrister giving the case summary due to Darren being unrepresented. The judge wanted to hear from

Darren and his reasons for going to court.

Darren immediately spluttered out his immature position with, "She took the kids from me last week and I have no idea where they are or how they are doing." The judge immediately jumped to conclusions which was completely unprofessional and started questioning the barrister about why the father didn't know where the children currently resided.

Rose had to whisper points to the barrister because how would he know every little in and out? Of course the police had advised not to give an address out due to risk of harm on her and the children. Rose was shaking like the last leaf of autumn clinging onto the branch on a windy day. She tried to breathe and didn't want Darren to see her state which was becoming unstable and panicky.

The judge couldn't see why the 'father' shouldn't know despite the advice Rose had been given, even if it was from the police. He was clearly a pro-father judge and Rose received a 'telling off' to which she could see Darren smirking. Rose couldn't bear to see this and she shuddered inside. In this moment Rose remembered how competitive Darren was.

* * *

I remember there were times of slight happiness in the relationship; it wasn't all doom and gloom. There were moments that cannot be denied no matter how few and far between they were, and most of them included the children in it. I've got to laugh looking back at some of these memories about how stupid they were or how ridiculous and I remember this moment which at the time wasn't so funny but looking back it made me laugh and realise just how pathetic Darren was.

We both were on the PlayStation 3; we were both big fans of gaming but really for me, it killed dead time. I had found this new game that was free to download and it was a bit like Bejewelled where you had to match three coloured items but you could move them across to each row to match. I had been playing on my own for a few rounds and realised there was a 2 player mode so as usual suggested to Darren to have a gaming session with me on it. Well, he just couldn't beat me no matter which way he tried, him starting or me, him changing a column, doing a different mode, and he was getting frustrated. I didn't realise he couldn't take losing with a pinch of salt like most of us do but he couldn't and a couple of hours had gone by and he still couldn't beat me. It was past midnight and we were still playing and I was starting to get really tired, the tired that you just need to drag yourself to bed or you will be asleep on the sofa, floor, toilet wherever you may be.

"OK, I'm really tired now so let's call it a day." I had suggested this as one of us always called it whenever it was just too tiring to carry on.

I didn't expect his snappy response, "Look, we're not going to bed until I beat you...and don't think about just letting me win."

I laughed as I thought he was joking and tired but he wasn't. "I'm being serious you know, it's pissing me off, it's a fucking stupid game anyway."

I didn't really know how to take Darren at times and this was one of them. I didn't know if he was going to turn around and generally laugh at the fact he was getting frustrated or if he was going to turn around and an awkward atmosphere would come.

I sat for half an hour because I knew that I couldn't let him win (or at least straight-away) but before I could pretend to fail, he completely lost the plot and stormed over to the PlayStation 3, grabbed it and yanked it hard so all the wires came out. He had this look of rage and he turned around and he lobbed it at the mirror on the wall. It smashed the mirror and the PlayStation 3 was clearly unplayable after this. I remember looking at him in shock and not knowing how to play it. I really wanted to laugh because it was like being in the room with a child.

I didn't realise Darren was super competitive, well I guess even more than that. I knew that it would then turn on me to be my fault, that I had wound him up and it would be my job to replace the PlayStation 3 and the mirror.

I guess it seems a bit silly when I think of this moment as a big deal but actually he broke my mirror that used to be my auntie's. I was very close to her and she had passed away the year before; this mirror was irreplaceable. Darren didn't care and didn't even mention it and I had learnt to be quiet.

* * *

The judge kept interrupting Rose's barrister and wanted to hear from Darren which was cringe-worthy for Rose as he put on this sob story and made out that he was the victim. He was good at manipulating a situation and clearly this was working on the judge; he would get a Masters' degree in manipulation if it was a qualification.

Rose's barrister eventually got to speak after the judge was empathising with the father. He didn't seem to care much about the Domestic Abuse within the statement or the fact Darren's family were aggressive and Rose had been thrown out. The judge kept hurrying the barrister on and he was trying to keep up and get the information across but the judge just didn't want to hear any of it...until finally...he came to the part where Rose had picked up the children and Harrison had been so ill he was hospitalised.

It was like the judge had had a Christmas present taken away from him, it was very surreal. The judge was then quick to say, "We need to pass this to the courts near where the children are currently residing and I suggest that they stay with their mother for the time being until the next hearing where we will schedule a longer session to decide the outcome of residency. This will be held within the next 3 months. There is to be access one day a week and the parents to discuss it outside of court with Barrister Redford."

Then the judge stamped his paperwork, didn't even look towards Rose or Darren and dismissed them out of the courtroom; they had come out the other end of the conveyer belt. Rose went back in the side room with the barrister and Darren went into his own side room on his own.

The barrister said to Rose, "I'll just go and see what Darren wants first because he is clearly going to be adamant on his choices and there is no point in us proposing anything first as it will be unsatisfactory to him."

Again the wait was a long one. Tim was asking Rose questions about what was said but Rose had a pounding headache and she could only hear static. Tim managed to snap her out of it and she told dribs and drabs of what went on but she was so dizzy and slurring her words. Rose got up from the chair and said, "I just need to get some water," but she lost her balance and fell to the ground.

CHAPTER THIRTEEN

I woke up on Lindsey's sofa and it was Christmas Eve. I hadn't seen her for over a year because I wasn't allowed to have a social life. I got up and dragged myself to the kitchen for some water; I had had a drinking session the night before and I had drunk more than I should. I thought it would take all my problems away and Tim wasn't around so I had to get out.

Last night Darren told me that I would only get to see the kids on Christmas Day for two hours. He gained full control over me by using the children. I handed over £1,000 to him which was the remainder of my money as he threatened I wouldn't see them at all. He claimed the money was for 2 months' rent and bills since we split up. Darren loved having control even more than before.

Now that he had thrown me out and had the children, he allowed me to have what he called 'access days'. He complained that I should be having them overnight once a week but I wasn't able to accommodate the children. I had nothing at the moment but it showed that he couldn't cope with the children full time and I could imagine that they were pining for me whilst I wasn't there.

The fact that Darren had thrown me out and it was a few days before Christmas was just as unbearable for me as it was for the kids. Darren had arranged that I could have the children for two hours in the morning of Christmas Day. It meant that I was to spend Christmas Day alone, I couldn't expect Tim to take the time off and I know he was meant to spend it with his family so I was feeling sorry for myself. I had no money to travel to see my parents after seeing the children and by the time I would be getting there I would be coming back. I had a measly 2 hours with Millie-Rose and Harrison. I had spent any money I had on giving Darren the £1,000 'debt' and I had to buy the kids some presents of course!

I couldn't even look at my phone and check my bank account; I had started waiting for the text alerts to say you have reached or are over your overdraft limit…but before that time came I went to the sink and threw up in it. Thank God the place looked like a dump already or I would have felt a little more guilty about having to now push potato and other veg found in my sick through the plug holes.

Normally, Lindsey would have been running in like the old days and puking up alongside me herself as she hadn't a strong stomach. But there was nothing.

I called her name to see if she was up. "Linsdeyyyyyy…" but nothing. I dragged my feet through the small living room and up the pink carpeted stairs. "Lindseyyyyy…" I whined out and I walked into her bedroom which was sick-pink all over but she wasn't anywhere to be found. I expected her to be scrunched up in her boudoir bed but it was neatly made and looked untouched.

I dragged myself to the bathroom where I puked again into the toilet; this time I got splash back and I was sick again, where did all this come from? I didn't remember eating loads last night. I allowed the wall to help me up and leant over the sink, slowly looking up to see what horror would appear in the mirror staring back. I looked disgusting and felt a failure of a mother. I had left those kids to live with him when I knew what he's like and what he'd done to them in the past…when will I see them? Two hours on Christmas Day isn't enough!

My eyes started to fill up and I couldn't control it; he had succeeded. I was feeling shit, with no one around me to help and no one would believe it if I told them anyway. I guess I had Tim, but he wouldn't really want landing with me with baggage, bringing him down to this mess.

I was starting to feel the urge to be sick again and put the cold tap on and put my neck under the tap and drank the ice cold water and then swelled my mouth out. I opened the cabinet above me and found paracetamol, the sickness had strained me and made my head throb hard…better to stop it now then let it get worse.

There were packets and packets of paracetamol in Lindsey's

medicine cabinet; God only knows why and I wasn't expecting the rush of opening them all up and swallowing all the tablets I could find…there were about 40. I didn't flinch or stall. I was one of those people who could just pop 5 tablets in my mouth and swallow in one go and not even need water. I looked in the mirror and thought that it felt better; he wouldn't have control over me anymore! I'd won!

My iPhone buzzed and I reached into my pocket and unlocked the screen showing me my beautiful children, so young and so innocent. I started to breathe fast and start to panic; the message was from Tim along with a few missed calls and a lot of unopened messages from him. I started to read them and my hand was now shaking.

'Hi Rose, what are you up to this evening? I know I said I wasn't free but there's been a change of plan. I know it's late but if you're free then give me a bell.'

I couldn't believe it, I bet he had changed his plans on purpose but I didn't want to burden him or for him to be with me for pity.

Then early this morning, *'Hey Rose, I had a message off your friend Lindsey to check on you, is everything ok?'*

I rolled my eyes, that girl is too caring for her own good. *'Rose, I've tried ringing you but no answer, I hope you're ok. Starting to get a bit worried about you as you never play hard to get like this with me :-).'*

The cheeky so and so! I couldn't help but giggle. "Shit," I suddenly thought…I started to look through the packets…how many tablets have I taken? I didn't feel any different but someone did care for me and wait… those kids need me! I've got to stop this…he is winning if I do this!

I started to shove my fingers down my throat to try and make myself sick, thankfully I was successful but there wasn't much to see but bile. I felt like a complete nutter. If someone saw me I reckon they would scoot me off to a mental hospital; how sad and pathetic was I. I couldn't let Tim find out… this could ruin everything! I had started to fully panic and my head was spinning. I couldn't concentrate on the phone screen. I tried to pull myself up from the toilet which had become my new friend. I stood up and completely lost balance and fell to the floor thumping my head on the way down and blacked out.

* * *

Rose was woken with a splash of water on her face and Tim was there with his parents; she came round fast and Tim gave her a kiss on the cheek. "It's the stress Rose, come on, it won't be long now, you don't want Darren knowing about this and thinking he has won; you're stronger."

Tim picked her up and placed her back in her seat. Thankfully the barrister wasn't back yet. Tim's mum had a stash of snacks in her handbag and handed Rose a chocolate bar. "You haven't eaten this morning love, eat this and the sugar will do you good."

Rose accepted it as she was being polite (she had only known Tim's parents a few weeks) and she forced half a bar down within a minute. It was very much welcomed.

Tim and his parents didn't push for what happened and waited for the barrister to come back in. They would wait to see what he had to say and find out what was going on. Eventually he dawdled back in to the room; he had taken his time, and sat down next to Rose and said, "Ok, Darren would like access to be on a Friday 11-5 and would like you to drop them off to his home in York and likewise to your home in Liverpool."

Rose was breathing deeply; she didn't realise that she had started to hyperventilate but Rose was starting to panic at the thought of him coming near her home.

Tim spoke for her, it was like he knew what was going through her mind, "I don't think going to either home is an option considering the domestic violence (DV) mentioned; I think it would be best to meet in a public place instead and I think Rose would feel better with this too."

Rose nervously nodded and got out a few words, "I'm...not feeling...too good...my head...is splitting. I don't care...about it...being on a Friday...and those times....let's give...him that...be amicable."

Tim placed his hand on her back and was rubbing it lightly; Rose felt instantly a rush of calm and warmth. She loved how Tim was so affectionate as it was something she hadn't had for years. Tim knew her so well to be able to talk for Rose and show this much concern. The barrister agreed and spoke it aloud as he wrote it on his note paper in a formal structure and said he would go and speak to Darren to confirm.

It didn't take long to confirm that Darren had agreed but asked for the meeting place to be at a corner shop just down the road from his home. Rose knew how rough it was and it wasn't an ideal place to meet. She personally didn't want to stand on any turf near Darren because of how close his family lived and his friends too (visions of his friends jumping them on a dark winter's night flashed into Rose's mind; her anxiety levels were not great and she imagined the worst).

Tim made a suggestion that they meet at a large superstore just on the outskirts of York but also within walking distance for Darren seeing as he didn't drive.

The barrister went back like a piggy in the middle. Rose thought to herself how sad it was that they could not just sort this out and that they had to have a referee (visions came into her head of them having a talking stick and the barrister passing it to each of them and telling the other off when talking without the stick – yes it seemed they were children themselves).

Eventually, after a lot of going back and forth with the barrister as a messenger, there was a rough plan in place; the barrister had to write out a rough court order and explained that if it wasn't neat handwriting the judge could dismiss it. He was rambling on about all these fussy and particular requests in the system as he was writing this order out. Rose felt like she was a second class citizen at this stage and that she thought the judge treated her as if she was one and that it was 'normal' for her to attend court like the 'rest of them'. Rose had all these emotions taking over her; she was having a fight with herself about it and thinking, 'but I come from a working class family and I run my own business. I decided to have my children, they weren't 'accidents' and I love them dearly'.

Rose didn't want to have to go back into the courtroom and see this judge who looked down his nose at her but she had no choice; the butterflies in her tummy had started again and she swore they had spikes on their wings because she felt sick, so sick she was yellow. Their names were spoken over the tannoy and away she walked, leaving Tim and his parents behind. They all gave her a nervous smile of encouragement and she took a deep breath, threw up in her mouth and bitterly swallowed it, and took a swig from the bottle of water that Tim had given her. Rose could tell that Tim, his parents and her friend were just as nervous for her but the difference was that they hid it better than her.

Rose remembered back to Christmas Day, the 2 hours of time she was allocated on Christmas Day.

***

It was a warm Christmas Day and the limited two hours went so fast and were so sad. We were stuck in a small rundown cheap hotel room and sat on my single bed. I tried my hardest not to cry and held my breath not to let a single tear drop down; I had the biggest lump in my throat and I felt drained. Millie-Rose kept asking me when they would be staying with me or when I would be coming back. Harrison wouldn't leave my side and was very quiet and solemn. I had an ache in my heart the whole time and even though they pined for me they lapped up every moment of our two hours.

It was the worst Christmas I had ever had and I had many a bad Christmas before. I had barely any gifts for them as the money I had was soaked up by the hotel room and the £1,000 Den had demanded. He had clearly done this so that I had nothing for them. I managed to scrape some pennies together and I got some toys from the charity shop, I never realised what a God-send that would be; how I value them now when before I would not even take a glance or consider taking a step inside. To be honest they didn't need that many gifts, they spent the whole time hugging me close and it made it unbearable for me.

Soon enough it was time to take the kids back. I thought about keeping them with me but I knew he would come after me and I couldn't keep them in a single-bed hotel room. Harrison alone would get poorly with his chest. I reluctantly dropped them both back off to their father who had a huge grin on his face and I felt he was like a pig in shit, he was having his moment.

I drove back to the hotel I was staying at for a few nights until my money would run out. I went in with my head down, unlocked the door to my room with difficulty and shut it behind me. Then I fell to the floor and cried. I could feel my heart breaking, being smashed, being ripped into little pieces, being trodden on. I had to try and think it was going to be ok but how was it going to be ok? I had to think this wasn't going to be forever, but I couldn't, what was going to happen to my beautiful innocent children who had no clue as to what was really happening. I spent half an hour sobbing away and feeling sorry for myself; my head was thumping and I wished I had a bottle of vodka to drink it away. I wasn't much of a drinker but maybe now was the time to take it up.

I had started to crawl along the floor in the attempt to climb into bed and cry myself to sleep when there was a knock on my hotel room door. I thought it was someone making a mistake and knocking at the wrong room. I quickly ran to the olive green sink in the olive green shower room and splashed my face with water, dabbed it with the cream hotel towel (which I believed used to be white) and unlocked the door. To my utter shock and surprise it was Tim! He was stood there in a suit and with a bunch of flowers...well, I cried even more! Cried firstly because I couldn't believe it and felt happy and then I thought I should be crying at what he was looking at: I bet I looked disgusting.

I told him off firstly, "You're meant to be with your family."

Tim simply and smoothly smiled back at me and said, "No one deserves to be alone on Christmas Day, especially you."

Could he have made me swoon anymore? I didn't know what to say but he welcomed himself in to my embarrassment of a hotel room. He didn't even look at anything else but me, as if I was the most beautiful woman in the world. Tim told me I was to get my glad rags on and that he was taking me out for a 5-course meal. He had clearly planned this and worked his magic, as how on earth would he get us booked in for a meal at such short notice and on Christmas Day? He made me feel so special; he made me feel alive again and he tried his upmost to make this day bearable and he didn't have to.

I did as he asked and I didn't try and tell him otherwise. He didn't rush me and I tried to slap as much makeup on as I could so I didn't look like a washed out ghost.

Tim replied to his emails and eventually I came out of the shower room with the one dress I had in my possession, a tie-around-the-neck, long brown dress with gold glitter shimmering down like a river. Tim's eyes lit up when he looked up from his iPhone. He led me out of the door and treated me like I was a true lady of elegance.

* * *

Rose felt a rush of warm feelings thinking about how Tim was so supportive from such a horrible situation. It made her lift her chin and push her shoulders back; she walked into the courtroom as confident as she could knowing that no matter what would happen, Tim would be waiting for her when she walked back out.

It turned out that Rose wasn't gone long and she even held the door open for Darren on the way out, her confidence beaming out of her. She was happy with the outcome and she wanted to feel in control for once. Rose informed Tim and his parents when she came out that it was simply a case of both her and Darren signing the draft court order having to adhere to it until the next court hearing. The judge let them leave with a few 'words of warning' on both of their parts and Rose couldn't stand the fact that the judge was making assumptions and saw past everything that Rose had built up to say in confronting Darren at the same time.

"Don't use the children as weapons because it will come back to bite you both when they are older and these children deserve to have the best upbringing they can."

Rose had found it very hard to keep her mouth shut and not speak back to the judge but if she could she would have told him exactly what she thought, 'You have no idea who I am, what I do, what kind of person I am, how much I love my children and I am the victim of HIS (pointing toward Darren) abuse which has led me into this court! Do you really think I would be here if it wasn't for him? I am not 'that' type you're describing. Not everyone who walks through your courtroom doors is an un-respectable person'. Rose had bitten her lip hard to not speak these words out loud.

Tim shook the barrister's hand before he left and thanked him. The barrister came to shake Rose's hand too and told her he would email the draft and also her solicitors' with the proceedings and a load more formal jargon that Rose pretended to understand. Rose took a huge sigh and had a big hug with Tim; this was a small step in the right direction.

Tim walked out of the front door of the courts with Rose in his arms. Rose had tears rolling down her cheeks and was trying to hold it together to be able to climb into Tim's dad's car and let it go. Rose didn't want Darren to see her at all, her reaction, her in general. She wanted her life to finally be private and happy. Rose climbed into James' car and she closed the door and began to wail. It was like someone had been playing on her heart strings like anchors hitting them. She felt the sinking feeling in her stomach, it was now grumbling in pain as she hadn't eaten.

Tim got tissues out of her handbag and said, "It wasn't ever going to be easy, but we are one step closer, you should look at this like a victory, part of the battle is won." There was a short silence. "Rose, I'm so proud of you! For facing it and having to be open about what happened to you."

Rose suddenly started giggling, "I wouldn't have done it without you, don't you see? You've been the one to show me how to stand up for myself and that I have no choice but to be true to my side because it depends on where the children will be." They both hugged and Rose left a wet patch on his suit jacket. Rose added, "No one has ever told me they are proud of me and it means so much to hear it from someone who truly believes in me and cares for me and loves me…I cannot thank you enough."

Tim said, "Let's get back to my parents' house; they have champagne waiting. I suggest you ring your mum and dad too." James and Sarah climbed into the car after paying the car parking charge and gave words of encouragement but Rose hadn't sussed Tim's parents out yet and was more worried about what they thought of who she was currently married to and who their son was with now. Trash? That's what she thought would be running through their minds.

Hugs welcomed Rose as they got back to his parents' house after a very silent car journey back. Rose felt a mixture of sickness and very drowsy to the point that she was nearly nodding off. She felt like she had been a part of Tim's family for years, they were so kind and accepting despite Rose doubting it herself. Rose rolled out some more tears, but it was worth the fight, it was worth everything to her, this was her life.

CHAPTER FOURTEEN

Tim's parents had invited a couple of family members and close friends over to their house to welcome them home. Rose was thinking it was peculiar making a fuss. What would have happened if she hadn't have got the answer she was looking for? But she stopped those thoughts because Rose felt a sense of freedom from an entrapment she had lived with for the past 6 years. The divorce would come, yes, but this was a fight for a beginning and a long journey awaited the end. They all climbed out of the car and were welcomed by a small crowd of people Rose had never met before. Suddenly Rose's mind felt a shifting from the court to the daunting factor of meeting Tim's family.

Soon champagne corks were going and cheering was happening as she rang 'round her family and enjoyed a few glasses at the end of the phone too. Rose was drinking her champagne and feeling a little light-headed. Tim was topping up her glass and everyone else's for that matter. It felt like a blunt end to the first battle in the war that was to come, but for Rose the biggest step and the most challenging was to face Darren and to tell the truth to the judge without letting his threats overcome her.

Emotionally drained was close to how Rose felt but the champagne helped. Her adrenaline was still high and coming down very slowly. It felt odd to Rose that everyone was drinking champagne and that everyone knew what had happened to her. She felt embarrassed, but looking around, she felt like she was at home.

Tim went over to Rose, who was daydreaming, and said, "Another top up?"

Rose grinned at Tim, sighed and replied, "Go on then, I'm just going to nip to the loo. I won't be a minute." Rose went upstairs and straight to the toilet where she was sick. She immediately felt better and then put her head under the tap at the bathroom sink and washed out her mouth. Rose thought champagne would wash the taste out and wasn't going to let Darren ruin anything else in her life. Tim was waiting for her as she came down the stairs and asked if she was ok. He handed her another glass of champagne and had a dish of salted peanuts. It reminded Rose of New Year's Eve.

Tim gave her a kiss on the cheek as she passed and placed his hand on her lower back to guide her into the celebrations. His mum and dad were looking over at them smiling and Rose was wondering what she had missed and went over to say her thank you's now that she had stood herself up straight and got her act together. "Thank you so much, Sarah," and Rose gave Tim's mum a hug and a kiss on the cheek. "Thank you, James, you don't know how much this all means to me," and Rose gave Tim's dad a hug and a kiss on the cheek.

Sarah beamed at Rose and said, "Look, this is what our family is about and this is what we do; it was a pleasure to help and thank you for letting us."

Rose interrupted, "But you shouldn't have to and you've done so much more than I had ever expected from you. I guess I am trying to say to you that you have only known me for such a short time but you have put everything aside and treat me like you have known me for years."

Sarah interrupted back. "Now come on…you don't need to say it, let's enjoy celebrating and have a break from thinking about it all."

Rose smiled, "Yes, you're right." Tim then clinked his glass to get everyone's attention. Rose was thinking, what on earth is he doing making this fuss!

"Can I have everyone's attention, please?" Rose had already started to blush. She hadn't even got the chance to talk to James' and Sarah's family and friends yet.

"Hi, everyone. I know you're all busy and are wanting to grab Rose for a chat…but I felt I had to just say a couple of words.

Firstly, thank you to my parents, whose footsteps I will continue to walk in as they are selfless and not at all frivolous when I came to them and explained whom I had met and that I needed to help her, but with their support." Rose was bright red and suddenly was filled with guilt and shame. "When they met Rose, which wasn't that long ago at all, they could see what I see and that's a beautiful young woman who loves to work hard and puts everyone else before herself." Rose's ears started to turn pink and she was shaking her head. "I would like us all to raise a glass to her because today she deserves to be celebrated as she put herself way outside her comfort zone and I can't tell you just how courageous this lady is. Let's raise a glass to Rose."

Rose was all bashful as everyone held up their champagne flutes and said, "To Rose!" in unison and took a swig of their champagne. Rose then followed and slightly raised her flute with a thank you grin and went to take a sip when something touched her lips that wasn't the champagne. Rose looked confused and curious, and she looked into her glass. Rose paused and wondered what on earth was going on; she could see a glint and a sparkle other than the bubbles of the champagne.

Tim had come up to her and gave Rose a look that Rose knew was his sign to say, 'everything will be ok' to her. He slowly got down onto one knee. Everyone around them were in complete silence watching Rose's every reaction; she was speechless.

Tim held her hand and looked up at her. "Rose, I don't know the half of what you have been through but I know that you are an incredibly brave woman; you never deserved to have been treated that way. I want to help you forget the pain and find happiness. I want to be the person that helps you stand up when you can't. I want to be the person you can confide in and trust unlike what you have had before. I am absolutely amazed by you as a person; you are not only intelligent, creative and hard-working but you're the most beautiful woman I have ever met."

Rose was welling up and shaking her head. She didn't believe what Tim was saying. "You may shake your head but I want to help change that. I want to help you see all the things I see in you and build your self-confidence up because you should be proud of yourself and the person you are. I must now say that above all of this you're a mum and your two children are so lucky to have you; they are such wonderful children and you have protected them since they were born and now they show a credit to you. If you will let me I want to get to be a part of your family and I want to help you protect them in the days, weeks, months and years to come. I see your love for them and it pours out and is infectious."

Rose had now uncontrollable tears rolling down her face and Tim hadn't taken his eyes off her; everyone around was transfixed on them both and could see the connection between them.

"So, if I may take your hand." Rose blushed, wiped her tears with one hand and gave her other hand to Tim, who took the ring from Rose and got ready to slip it onto her hand. "Rose Stephanie Shaw…will you let me join you on your journey and will you marry me?"

Rose looked around at all of Tim's family expecting someone to stop him from making a stupid mistake but they all smiled at her. Rose took a deep breath and didn't want to hesitate, she knew the answer to the question but there was a pause because it was tarnished with her previous relationship and she thought about what if she got back into another situation like what she had just escaped? She told herself she would give time with Tim and it was vital she and her children were safe. Rose thought back and remembered what it was like in the beginning of her relationship with Darren.

* * *

I was getting ready for a night out with my new boyfriend. I planned for my girlfriends and his mates to get together with us. I had spent an hour curling my thick red hair and I probably put too much makeup on. I had my tunes on loud and was already starting to have a drink with Darren; he had spent most of his time smoking cigars (he had them on the odd occasion as a treat) and drinking whiskey straight whilst I stopped in front of the mirror above the mantelpiece making stupid face expressions whilst applying the mascara. Once I was ready, I looked stunning and it was the only time I felt worth something, I had these amazing stiletto heels that must have been 6 inches and made my legs look even longer and a very short dress that flared out slightly and a high waist line with a graphic punch of a design. I always liked taking a few photos which would be fab for Instagram which I seem to have rather a following on. I gave a few poses and was really happy with how I looked. I turned to Darren and I simply said, "How do I look?" thinking he would do his usual knocked off the seat humour by being gobsmacked by my supposed beauty. He had done this every time we had gone out before.

This time wasn't quite the reaction I had hoped for; he was half-arsed and hummed in approval. I asked him, "Is everything ok?" and went to sit on his lap. Darren wasn't best pleased with me doing that with his cigar in his mouth, his whiskey in one hand and his phone in the other which he didn't take his eyes off. Den stopped me from sitting on his lap and I thought I had done something wrong. I sat next to him and checked my own phone to see where my girls were and waited patiently for him to not be busy on his phone. A half hour had passed and my friends had told me they had set off for the pub.

"Den, Lindsey and everyone have said they are just getting into their taxi, are we ready?" and Darren seemed to shake himself together and said, "Yep...sorry...I was in my own world there."

I was baffled but still asked him, "So, what do you think?" and I got up and gave him a twirl.

Darren looked at me and gave a smile and remarked, "Yes, you look great, as usual of course."

I still wasn't satisfied as usually his jaw was on the floor but I gave him a huge smile and went to put a kiss on his lips but he started laughing. I glanced in the mirror thinking I must have a makeup smudge or my hair was a mess but I saw nothing. "What's funny, Den?" Perhaps I missed something.

He came over to me and put his hand on my shoulder and was kneeling with laughter and looked up at me and said, "I never realised just how big your smile was." I was even more confused thinking this may be a good thing? I said nothing and he got up and put his hand on my cheek. "You have a beautiful smile, it's huge. But it's so big I hadn't noticed before; you look like you have a joker smile – you know like Heath Ledger in the Dark Knight. He cut the sides of his mouth so that he was always smiling," and he laughed again. "Sorry, I can't look at you right now, that's all I see."

I was completely confused and upset, why would he say something like this? I wasn't going to get myself too upset about it but I told him he was a twat in my head. I didn't quite know how to voice it. "I'm just going to the bathroom before we go." I thought I better go and look for myself at what was so hilarious.

That moment I felt something wasn't right; there's taking the mick and then there's someone laughing AT you. It didn't sit right and I automatically became self-conscious.

Later in the night, we were on our way home and I was walking with my girlfriends. We had all clearly drank too much and we were enjoying our time shouting to each other as if we were miles away because of that buzz in your ear after spending time in a bar. We had racked up to our favourite take-away where the staff knew us all by name; it must have been around 4am. Darren was with his mates and we kept catching each other's eye and kept on blowing kisses to one another and winking. We loved to flirt with each other.

We had queued up for the take-away and the guys had gone first. The ladies were still shouting to each other what we were up to and laughing at meaningless things. I was the last to order and the security guard moved me on to the other side of the take-away as I was leaning on the counter like it was my pillow. I had got up the energy to move with his assistance when Darren came flying in, ready to fight this very tall, masculine man who you would not mess with. I didn't really know much of what was going on but when I got pulled by my girlfriends out of the take-away and without my cheesey chips, I was rather disappointed. I was linked to Lindsey and she was keeping me upright. We walked out to see the security guard thumping Darren in the gut and clearly winding him. Darren's friends were picking him up and telling him to walk on and apologised for him. I had no idea what was going on at all.

Lindsey walked up to Darren's friends with me and I said, "What's… going on?" I stalled as I hiccupped half way through my question.

Mike, who was one of Darren's best friends, had sobered up. "I don't really know, I just know it was something to do with you and that security guard." I was baffled and went over to Darren to see if he was ok; he was coughing and I put my arm round him – he shrugged me off quite harshly and gave me this stern look that said, 'I will never forget'.

Mike intervened and told me it was best to let him walk Darren home and for me to stay over at my friends'. I reassured Mike that everything was ok and if he helped me to the top of the street we would be fine from there. Darren didn't speak to me or even look at me the whole way home. Mike sure enough left us at the top of the street and Darren had perked up and didn't want my assistance the last of the way home. I just stayed silent as I didn't know what to say. I took the house key out of my clutch bag and unlocked the door. Darren shoved his way past me.

Once I shut the door, he then spoke, "I can't believe you!" He shouted at me like I had done something horrendously wrong.

I was a bit stumped and said, "Why...what?" Darren was shocked that I didn't know. He went through his pockets and got out a cigar and lit it, took a drag and felt better. I was frozen on the spot and didn't know what I should do or how to talk to him but thought I would still try, "Well, I had a good night. It was funny when Lyndsey and Mike were on the pole wasn't it?" and I laughed nervously.

Darren didn't seem to go along with me and laugh. In fact, he was starting to get angry and raised his voice more. "So, when that security guard came up to you, you thought you would let him get away with it?"

I was wondering what on earth he was talking about and clearly had a gormless face.

"Come on...you must know what I'm talking about especially as you liked it." Again, I had no idea and Darren took a long drag of his cigar and walked towards me and blew all the smoke to the side. I just stood there, he looked me right in the eye and said, "You will never look at another man like that ever again! You are MY girlfriend and only I can look at you." He was getting closer to me and his nose was nearly touching mine. "Do you understand?" I nodded vigorously at him. "Well, come on...DO YOU UNDERSTAND?" and he shouted in my face.

With no hesitation I said, "Yes." I couldn't say no, could I? But, that wasn't good enough.

"I don't believe you," and suddenly I felt something hot and sharp on the top of my shoulder. I went to scratch it and I saw Darren take his cigar off me and he said, "You're mine," and he walked away.

I was left gritting my teeth and sounding like a snake as I tried to keep calm but it stung so bad and was all red, the smell was hideous. I waited until Darren was out of sight and I went to the kitchen sink and put my shoulder under the cold tap which proved difficult and meant me having to bend in a way that I shouldn't be able to bend. I spent the next hour under the tap to try and sooth the pain and I sobbed. I had no idea why on earth he would want to do this.

* * *

Everyone was still looking at Rose as she came out of her own world and she saw Tim looking up at her like a lost puppy waiting for her response. Rose had a sudden moment of realisation. She had figured it out. 'I was branded, branded like I was his possession, his object, his everything', Rose thought to herself and went to feel the top of her shoulder; she could feel the scar and held back her breath. Rose kept thinking, 'Tim hasn't told me I am his, he has said I can do what I would like and he wants to support me and the children', a tear crept out of her eye and slid down her cheek and then she felt a warm rub on her hand and looked down. It was Tim stroking her hand. Rose could feel the warmth from his hand flow up her arm and was followed with pins and needles and butterflies all in one. She had never felt like this – felt like someone cared, loved, and would give up everything for her. Tim was affectionate and it was what was missing from her life. Rose began to feel happy and she hadn't felt anything like it before; she had forgotten what it was like to feel happy.

Slowly she knelt down and joined Tim on the floor and held his hand back, "I will marry you but not only that, I want to promise you that I will try, I will try to find refuge within myself so that you aren't shadowed by my past. This won't be easy and I ask that you are patient with me. I know I need to believe in myself and believe in you, I have no reason to doubt you and so I will try my best not to."

Rose helped Tim put on the ring, a simple and elegant one diamond with a platinum band which complemented Rose like it was made for her. Tim had tears in his eyes and Rose had them rolling down her face, both with the widest smiles in the room. They both giggled and that was everyone's cue to applaud and cheer. Tim leant towards Rose, still kneeling on the floor and kissed her lips tenderly. They both rose from the ground still embracing with a kiss which slowly turned into a hug. Rose felt the warm embrace of his security and let him hold her. Tim's family came huddling around them and cuddling them like one big pile-on; they all believed in them as a couple and were there ready to support them.

Tim and Rose shared a glass of champagne and Rose thought it was best to mention something she thought Tim hadn't considered. "You have to ask the children for their approval yet, you know?" Tim's face went from wide-smile to concerned and they both laughed together.

Rose said, "Don't worry, they already love you and I think they would love to have you as their step-dad."

Rose giggled again thinking Tim will have not thought of the word 'dad' but he smiled back and said, "Rose, I can't wait to start," and he kissed her on the lips. "Now, let's get everyone drunk in celebrating with us; you haven't seen my mum when she's had a few – it's a good job there's no karaoke."

Rose giggled again, looking over at his mum who was already hiccupping and on her fifth glass of champagne. She looked around and could see smiles and celebration all around her; family and friends who were supportive and cared. It was all she had ever wanted. Tim was all she had ever wanted. Amongst this mess, she had found the love of her life and she hoped that everything would work out fine. Wouldn't it?

ACKNOWLEDGEMENTS

Thank you firstly to Susan Miller from All Words Matter who not only edited this book but has been a friend before and during the making of this book. Thank you for your direction with the sensitive side of this novel.

Thank you to Georgina Preston from Savannah Rose Digital Imaging who edited the video content for the Kickstarter campaign to fund the release of the book, and also assisted with the cover design and under a tight time frame.

Thank you to Judy Gilmour who not only assisted greatly with the press releases but who is my very much loved mother-in-law. Thank you for believing in me and my vision and for your ongoing support, love and care. You are an amazing woman and you constantly look out for your family and friends.

And thank you to my fellow authors who have taken their time out of their busy schedules to help, guide and support me.

Thank you to those who supported by pledging in the Kickstarter campaign which took place July and August 2016. Without your support, the vision would have been restricted and you were the first to stand with me and begin to block the road to Isolation Junction.

Thank you to the following people who pledged their support:

Amanda McCormick
Beat Mueller
Becka Simm
Beckie Brothers
Biddie Atkinson
Burt Jarratt
Claire Capper
Dawn Melbourne
Debbie Mawer
Denise Allen
Dianne Woodford
Gill Botterill
Hannah Maiden
Heather Benstead
Irene Furber
Jackie Woolnough
Jan McKinley
Jenna Jones
Jo Howarth
Joanne Jamieson
John Redhead
Jude Lennon
Judith Gilmour
Julie Aldcroft
Justyna Cieslinska
Linda Harper
Linda Mulholland
Lisa Preston
Lisa Southall
Mary Osborne

Michala Leyland, Wood for The Trees Coaching
Michele Stevenson
Michelle Emma Ogborne
Michelle Peters
Nicci Simmonds
Nicky Bartley
Paul Harper
Robin Gilmour
Sandra Bingley
Sarah Brock
Sharon Bosker
Sharon Kearns
Stacey Gales
Stephanie Hemsted
Sue Blaylock
Suze Dunkling - Ellie Harvey Silver
Suzie Oulton
Tammy Middleton
Vicki Sparks

ABOUT THE AUTHOR

Born in the North East, Jennifer is a young, married mum with three children. In addition to being an author, she is an entrepreneur, running a family business from her home-base. Her blog posts have a large readership of other young mums in business.

From an early age, Jennifer has had a passion for writing and started gathering ideas and plot lines from her teenage years. A passionate advocate for women in abusive relationships, she has drawn on her personal experiences to write this first novel. It details the journey of a young woman from the despair of an emotionally abusive and unhappy marriage to develop the confidence to challenge and change her life and to love again.

A MESSAGE FROM THE AUTHOR:

I hope that in reading my book, I will raise awareness of this often hidden and unseen behaviour and empower women in abusive relationships to seek help for themselves and find the confidence to change their lives.

If you have been affected by what you have read in this book, you are not alone, talk to someone and take the first step out of isolation. Or you can call the 24 hour free-phone National Domestic Violence helpline on 0808 2000 247.

There are national and local charity and council-led helplines, so I urge you to make that call, if it's safe.

If you are not in the UK I am sure there are support lines of a similar nature.

Jennifer

www.JenniferGilmour.com
www.facebook.com/IsolationJunctionbook
www.twitter.com/JenLGilmour

Made in the USA
Charleston, SC
26 September 2016